About the author

Ajay K Pandey grew up in the modest NTPC township of Rihand Nagar with big dreams. He studied Engineering in Electronics at IERT (Allahabad) and MBA at IIMM (Pune) before taking up a job in a corporate firm.

He grew up with a dream of becoming a teacher, but destiny landed him in the IT field. Travelling, trekking and reading novels are his hobbies. Travelling to different places has taught him about diverse cultures and people, and makes him wonder how despite all the differences, there is a bond that unites them. Trekking always inspires him to deal with challenges like a sport. Reading is perhaps what makes him feel alive.

You are the Best Wife is his debut book based on his life events and lessons. Apart from writing, he wants to follow his role model Mother Teresa and create a charitable trust to support aged people and educate special children.

After his debut book *You Are the Best Wife*, Ajay has authored bestselling titles like *Her Last Wish, You Are the Best Friend, Everything I Never Told You, An Unexpected Gift, A Girl to Remember* and *The Girl in the Red Lipstick.*

 *: AuthorAjayPandey*  *: @AjayPandey_08*

 *: @author_ajaykpandey*  *: ajaypandey0807@gmail.com*

YOU ARE THE BEST WIFE

The true story that touched lakhs of hearts

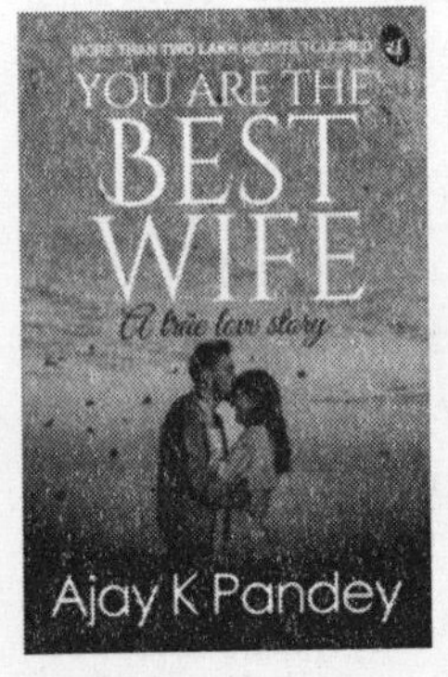

Ajay and Bhavna are very different people when they meet in college. As love blossoms, they have to brave all challenges, including their families.

A true story of how love can make you do extraordinary things, read this book to witness Ajay and Bhavna's journey that inspires to live fully, laugh heartily and enjoy each moment to the fullest.

First published in 2015, this book went on to become a bestseller soon after. It is based on the author's real life story and made it straight to the hearts of his readers. It is still one of the rare titles to retain 4.5 stars after close to ten thousand reader reviews.

You can also read this heart-touching bestseller in Hindi, Marathi and Chinese.

I Wish I Could Tell Her

Be the reason
Someone Smiles

Ajay K Pandey

Ajay K Pandey

Srishti
PUBLISHERS & DISTRIBUTORS

Srishti Publishers & Distributors
A unit of AJR Publishing LLP
212A, Peacock Lane
Shahpur Jat, New Delhi – 110 049
editorial@srishtipublishers.com

First Published by Srishti Publishers & Distributors in 2022

10 9 8 7 6 5 4 3 2

This is a work of fiction. The characters, places, organisations and events described in this book are either a work of the author's imagination or have been used fictitiously. Any resemblance to people, living or dead, places, events, communities or organisations is purely coincidental. The term "black" is used to highlight the pertinent issue of discrimination based on colour and to generate awareness about it in the society. The intent is not to hurt the sentiments of any individual or social group.

Printed and bound in India

The book is dedicated to my friend

who uses a lot of filters

while posting pictures on Instagram.

I wish I could name you, but I can proudly say that

you are exceptionally beautiful, even without these filters.

Your simplicity is your true beauty.

'If a good-looking face was the definition of beauty, then no one would love their ailing mother and a wrinkle-faced father.'

– *Radhika*

A note from the author

The notion of writing this book germinated when I was reading a matrimonial advertisement for my cousin years ago. I was surprised to notice how racist they were! They seemed to glorify fair-skinned people. My mind was filled with a number of questions:

Why does everyone want a fair-skinned partner on Indian matrimonial sites?

Why do dark-skinned people feel the need to apply filters before posting their pictures on social media?

Why do we rarely find dark-skinned air hostesses?

Why do we always choose a fair-skinned girl for the role of an angel in school plays?

Why are the statues of gods and goddesses so fair and beautiful?

Vasu's story is an attempt to address these issues, which have been lingering in my mind for years. Through this book, I intend to bring into light the perspective of those who have been treated *unfairly* by the society.

I want to offer my respect and support to you all.

You are no less than anyone!

Acknowledgment

A big thank you to my readers for accepting my crazy stories.

I am more active on Instagram (@author_ajaykpandey) and Twitter, so please do connect. I try with all my heart to reply to every message and comment that I get. Believe it or not, you have made me what I am today.

My deep respect to my entire family, that stood by me and decided to take each step with me.

Heartfelt gratitude to the exceptional team at Srishti Publishers for their superb guidance. A special mention to Jayant Bose, Arup Bose, Stuti and Vini Bhati.

Thanks Jasmeet Walia, for being the first reader and for your initial contribution to the book.

Your reviews and feedback are the silent, but efficient ways to enrich an author. So please keep pouring love, like you always do.

More than anything else, thank you for making me an author, though I would always politely ask you to treat me as your "author friend".

Never surrender!
Ajay K Pandey

1

Poster Boy

It was the summer of 1998. Pink City Jaipur was burning at 43.2 degrees Celsius, the hottest day of the season. The students of Court Secondary School were gearing up for their upcoming summer camp.

As I walked out of the school washroom, I noticed three pairs of eyes on me. When my eyes met theirs, they immediately pretended to be busy reading the notice board. There were bizarre smiles on their faces and their giggles echoed in the entire corridor. The mockingbirds were Sanjay, Pankaj and Alisha.

I ignored them and walked towards the class. I saw several other students sniggering while scanning the notice board. As soon as they saw me, I became their laughingstock. My mind spiralled with confusion.

'Vasu, you are on the notice board,' Tina ma'am said while crossing the aisle.

'Oh really?'

I checked the notice board, the crowd now thinning around it. I saw my photo, next to my classmate Pankaj's. It was an announcement about the upcoming summer camp. The caption read:

Be a smart student and join the summer camp.

The text with my picture was:

He did not attend the summer camp last year.

The text over Pankaj's photograph said:

The one who joined the summer camp.

I was looking my usual self, but Pankaj looked brighter. Before this, I had only seen posters of film heroes. The last line of the poster read:

Hurry up! Enrol yourself at the earliest as we have limited seats. The first fifty registrations are eligible for a twenty percent early bird discount.

I scanned my surroundings to ensure no one was around. Then, I peeled off the poster, folded it and tucked it inside my pocket.

'My picture is on all the notice boards, yippee!' I screamed with excitement.

When the bell rang at the end of the day, I navigated my way through a horde of students to leave for home. I saw a few students giggling at the school gate and reciprocated with a smile.

I remembered my elder sister Kavya's words, 'Only a jealous person laughs at you.' I concluded that my sudden glory on the notice boards had made others envy me.

•

Kavya gave me a ride on her two-wheeler to school each morning. In the afternoon, I walked the one-and-a-half kilometres stretch till home.

But today, I was running with zest. I had unfolded the poster thrice. It was a big celebrity moment for me. I wondered which ice cream I should demand from my mother on this special day.

I reached home, jumping with joy. My mom was surprised and said, 'Hello Vasu! You look quite excited today.'

'Mom, my photo is up on every notice board in school.' I opened the A5 size poster and asked, 'How do I look?'

Mom glanced at the poster. She looked at me and then she compared the poster boy and me at least thrice. The smile on her face disappeared. She pursed her lips and became silent. I thought she hadn't understood the English captions with the pictures.

'Kavyaaa!' she screamed. I could not understand why she was calling my sister instead of congratulating me.

'Yes, mom?'

Mom gave Kavya a jarring look, handing over the poster to her. She looked at the digital print like an experienced pathologist and knitted her brows. Kavya read my face and understood what hid behind my silly smile.

'Did you understand what the poster is all about?' she questioned me.

'Of course! This shows that I am smart, even though I did not join the summer camp last year,' I exclaimed.

Kavya faked a grin and raised an eyebrow.

She sighed and looked at mom, who nodded back at Kavya.

'You are such a lucky boy, Vasu! Your picture is on every notice board,' Kavya said.

'Yes!' I replied cheerfully. 'I want to celebrate with an ice cream.'

'Why not! Go, freshen up! I want to talk to mom,' she said.

I nodded and headed inside. I was a few metres away from them now, but could hear them clearly.

'Let's go and meet the principal, Kavya?' mom said.

'She is not in the city for the next few days, mom.'

'Then who is answerable for this poster?'

'It must be the stupid cultural secretary of our school.'

'Keep a check on your words, Kavya. Your brother is here.' Mom looked at me and passed a genuine smile.

'Let's go, mom!' Kavya said gravely, as if the Third World War was about to begin. They got ready quickly and headed out as if going to the battlefield. Meanwhile, I scrutinized the poster yet again, but couldn't fathom why they were reacting this way.

'Give me that poster!' Kavya ordered.

'No, Kavya. Why are you jealous of me?'

She rolled her eyes at my frivolous question but maintained her composure.

'Because you are a handsome boy,' she said while patting my head. 'Now let's go!'

Kavya is four years elder to me, but she behaves like my mother sometimes. Shouldn't she be more chill?

She rubbed in the fact that she is older by occupying the king-size bed in the room we shared, as I was given a single bed. Even though she never shared her ice cream with me, I knew that she would go to any extent to support me. She was like a furious tigress in front of the world, but mellowed down in front of me. We fought often, but she was always my go-to person.

•

Mom and I sat pillion on Kavya's black Honda Activa. My mind was still occupied with the poster. I couldn't understand why we were going to school, but decided to remain silent. When we reached there, the security guard at the school gate stopped us.

'Where are you going?' he asked.

'I am a class X student,' she told the guard and showed her identity card.

He nodded and made way for us. 'Where can I find Anil sir?' Kavya asked.

'Who Anil? Sharma or Verma?'

'Anil Mishra, head of the cultural committee,' she emphasised.

'Staff room.'

We parked the two-wheeler and walked towards the staff room. Kavya stared intently at the notice board right outside the door. She peeped in, but the room was empty. So she peeled off the poster and asked in a loud voice, 'Where is Anil sir?'

'Which Anil? Sharma or Verma?' the school peon asked.

'Cultural secretary.'

'He should be in the auditorium.'

Kavya sprinted towards the auditorium, making me wonder why she was in such a hurry. Mom and I followed her quietly.

'Anil sir!' she shouted. I was stunned to see her anger.

'Why is she screaming?' I asked mom.

'You stay out of this, Vasu.'

The auditorium was empty, so we walked towards the green room. We finally saw Anil sir, scribbling something on a piece of paper.

'What is this, sir?' Kavya unfurled the poster on his desk.

'Could you please lower your voice? You cannot talk to me like this!' Anil sir roared back. I shivered a little.

'Don't you dare silence her!' This time, my mom echoed Kavya's fury.

'We need an explanation.' I stepped back to escape the awkwardness and sat silently on a chair in the corner as mom went on.

He read the poster and replied, 'What is wrong with the poster?'

Kavya pointed at me. Anil sir gazed at me and I acknowledged him with a smile.

'Is the black boy him?' Anil sir's voice changed.

'Don't call him that!' Kavya hissed in fury.

He swallowed uncomfortably and pressed his lips together. 'Sorry, actually I was not aware of all this. A student gave me this picture. I thought it was some random picture downloaded from the internet.'

'It is illegal to use someone's picture without their permission,' mom said.

'It's also racist to use it in a poster in this way,' Kavya said.

Racist! It was a new word for me.

Anil sir lowered his head and removed his spectacles. He drank a few sips of water and said apologetically, 'I will get all the posters removed right away.'

My heart sank on hearing this. I could not understand what was happening around me.

'Thank you!' said mom, more with attitude than gratitude.

'No, that is not enough,' Kavya said.

'I am sorry, Kavya. I can't do anything further.'

'If this reaches principal ma'am, I am sure she can do a lot.'

Anil sir flared his nostrils. His face stiffened and he clenched his fist.

'He has already apologised, Kavya. Let it go!' mom said.

'No, mom. That is not enough.'

'Please don't report to the principal. What do you want?'

Kavya flashed a victorious smile. 'There is a fashion show next month.' She signalled to me and I joined them.

'Who will decide the winner?' Kavya asked.

'A group of panellists,' Anil sir said reluctantly, not liking where the conversation was headed.

'No, this time *you* will decide the winner.'

'But what would you want from the fashion show?'

'You already have the winner of the fashion show.'

Kavya pulled me in front of Anil sir and said, 'Vasu, say "thank you, sir".'

'Thank you, sir,' I said with a smile, totally oblivious of the changing circumstances.

'It's impossible for me to do that...' Anil sir swallowed.

'Sir, I know principal ma'am does not like you a lot.'

2

The Fashion Show

August 1998
Class VI

The students were looking forward to the upcoming fashion show. There was a lot of hustle-bustle around me. Somehow, the excitement did not rub off on me. I continued sitting on the last bench, mostly by myself, except a few times during the class tests.

Our new class teacher, Vidya ma'am, had a unique way of welcoming new students. Whenever someone joined us, a student volunteer had to give a welcome speech on behalf of the entire class. A few new faces had joined my section in this session as well. After two Sachins and three Nehas, a girl named Radhika entered the class.

I could hear a few boys murmur 'Wow!' when they saw her. It was hard to see her properly from the last bench.

'Hello everyone! Let me introduce you to Radhika Chauhan. She is a new admission to our class. Can we have a welcome applause for her?'

The class echoed with claps, more intense than required.

'Now someone has to give a welcome speech on behalf of the class.' There was deadly silence as Ms Vidya looked through a few faces. Then, her eyes rested on me.

'Vasu, why don't you try?'

The girls sitting on the first bench giggled and Vidya ma'am gave them a stern look. I froze in my seat as I rarely spoke in the class. Mustering some courage, I stood up from my seat with a blank face.

'Come on, Vasu. Give it a try!'

I tried to open my mouth twice, but found no words to voice my ideas. I gulped and started sweating. My breath was heavy.

'Relax! You can be creative. There is no need to give a long and scripted speech. Take your time.' She moved to Radhika and said, 'Why don't you introduce yourself while Vasu is gathering his thoughts?'

Radhika started her long introduction, talking about her previous school, achievements and family background. My eyes flickered. I wondered how she was so fluent while it was so hard for me to utter even a single word. To me, she looked like a foreigner in her wavy, brunette hair, fair skin and tall frame.

I realized how I could make my welcome speech really special. I pulled out an A4 size paper and started writing.

The thing is, my father owned a travel and tourism company. He often went to the airport to welcome international tourists. I had noticed how everyone stood at the exit gate with a placard. On a few occasions, even papa welcomed the guests with a smile and a placard.

I decided to replicate that, so I signed my name at the bottom. Then I reread the placard, struck out ~~VASU~~ and wrote 'Section C' instead.

After Radhika finished speaking, everyone diverted their attention towards me. I walked towards Radhika and displayed the white paper. The classroom roared with laughter.

Vidya ma'am looked at me and gave me a comforting smile. She said, 'It's a creative way to welcome someone,' and signalled the students to clap for me.

I displayed the white sheet to Radhika.

WELCOME RADHIKA

~~VASU~~

SECTION C

She took the white sheet with a smile and said, 'Thank you, Vasu!'

'How do you know my name?'

'Why did you cut your name?' she replied.

I smiled.

•

What should I wear? What makeup will look good on me? Will high heels be better or long boots?

While the girls of the class were grappling with these pertinent questions close to the fashion show, the boys were speculating which girl could win the fashion show from our class. The preparations were on in full swing. I failed to understand why everyone was so excited to admire a bunch of people who would walk on the ramp, dressed in fancy clothes. This trend did not appeal to me.

The class had accepted Radhika quickly. There were always more boys than girls surrounding her. She sat a few rows away from me, but joined me on the last bench during boring lectures. She seldom remained attentive during those and dozed off.

Pankaj often teased me whenever we sat together. 'Black and white TV is still a hit!'

Radhika never laughed at Pankaj's jokes. Instead, she would sharply reply, 'Black and white movies are always romantic!'

•

Anil sir summoned me for an audition. Since I was awkward in presenting myself most of the times, he wasn't very impressed with my performance.

However, when I saw the list of ten shortlisted students for the fashion show on the notice board, I was surprised to see that only Radhika and I had qualified from our section.

There was a sense of disappointment looming large over the class. A few students were crying beyond consolation. Pankaj openly expressed his anger and kept asking, 'How come Vasu is there in the list?'

Some of them were so angry that they had even demanded an explanation from Anil sir.

'On which ground have you selected Vasu? It is unfair!' someone said.

But Anil sir did not pay heed to their allegations.

•

Two days before the fashion show, Anil sir enquired what I would be wearing for the fashion show. His frown was becoming more noticeable as we neared the day of the event. The resentment amongst my classmates regarding my selection was so intense that their parents had complained about this decision.

To our dismay, Anil sir made a major announcement, just a day before the fashion show. The circular on the notice board read:

> *Dear students,*
>
> *Every year, we decide a theme for the fashion show. For this year, the theme is 'Halloween'.*
>
> *Let us celebrate fashion together!*

Radhika was surprised. 'What is this? How am I going to shop at the last moment?' she said, almost crying.

I was consoling her by saying that she would ace the look when the peon called me to Anil sir's room. Sir gave me a series of instructions and then whispered, 'Come to me before the fashion show starts tomorrow.'

•

The most awaited day had finally arrived. All the participants had tried earnestly to dress up as stylishly as they could. Radhika was wearing a black gown, with a few red scary tattoos on her face which made her look adorable. I was becoming fond of this charming vampire.

In the meantime, I went to meet Anil sir. He scrutinized my dress and thought for a few seconds.

'Let me put some makeup on your face,' he offered.

I was amazed to see that the school's cultural secretary was personally assisting me in this way.

He put a few red spots on my cheeks and stepped back to see how it looked. 'Eh, it's not visible!' He tried the dark blue colour and then said. 'Even blue is not visible on your face!'

'Sir, try using white colour,' I suggested.

He smiled. 'Good boy,' he said as he applied a few dabs of white on my face. Even after that, he was not convinced. Then he dug into a bag on his table and applied a deep red colour on my lips. He glanced at me but rubbed the red away.

I understood that the colour was not visible, so I offered help. 'Sir, you can paint my teeth.'

'Yes, good idea!'

He did his work and examined me twice before saying, 'Now this is a winner's face.'

•

The fashion show had begun. The students were filled with exuberance as they were cheering vigorously for every participant.

The panellists of the fashion show were a group of teachers who were judging every performer on the basis of their level of confidence and presentation skills.

According to the format of the competition, a boy and a girl would be announced the winner in the end. Once the panellists submitted the scores, Anil sir would make the final count and declare the result. I was sad that Kavya would miss the show, since class ten students were busy with their extra classes.

I was waiting nervously in the green room when one of the student coordinators called my name. I had been hearing rounds of applause every now and then, welcoming contestants. Finally, I stepped out and walked on the ramp for the first time in my life, facing so many people. To my surprise, no one clapped and cheered for me. Undeterred by the disheartening response, I walked until the end and exhibited my red teeth. Seeing my courage, a few teachers gave me a sympathetic smile and applauded for me.

Anil sir joined them in their appreciation. His lips moving to say, 'Good boy!'

I finished my walk confidently and went backstage. There were a couple of more students after me, and then the show came to an end.

Finally, after waiting for about fifteen more minutes, the results were announced. It was the happiest day of my life.

Radhika and I were declared the winners of the Halloween King and Queen title. Even though not many people clapped to celebrate my victory, I was genuinely happy.

When we walked out of the auditorium, there were many people who wanted to click pictures with Radhika. It was no surprise that not many acknowledged my presence. I sat down in the corner to let the chaos settle. I was amused how a vampire could be so cute.

Radhika came to me and said, 'Vasu, come, get pictures with us. You are also the winner.'

'But no one wants to click a picture with me.'

'They want to get clicked with the winner. If I am the Halloween Queen, then you are the King.'

A voice inside me said, 'Wow, I am a king!'

I joined them as a few friends came to click pictures with us.

Suddenly Pankaj crossed us and Radhika shouted, 'Pankaj, do you want to get a picture with us?'

'I am not interested,' he replied.

'Seems black and white is still a hit!' Radhika and I chuckled.

•

I returned to the green room. Anil sir congratulated me and smiled. He gave me a tissue and said, 'Please wash your face and teeth.'

I cleaned everything, held the trophy in my hand and walked back home.

When I entered the house, I screamed with joy, 'I won the fashion show!'

Mom gave me a warm hug and my father praised me for my victory. To celebrate, we went out for dinner that evening where I gorged on my favourite dry-fruit ice cream.

When we got back home, I stood gazing at myself in the mirror for a long time. Kavya noticed this and said, 'Oh, handsome boy! What are you looking at in the mirror?'

'Kavya, I am wondering why I am dark and Radhika is fair.'

'Everyone is different, bro...'

'But why is Radhika so beautiful and I am not?'

She sat on her bed and said, 'Vasu, I want you to understand that every person is beautiful in their own skin.'

'That's not true. Look at her! She has such a good-looking face.'

Then, Kavya rose from her bed and stood behind me. Now we both were looking in the mirror. She pointed at the mirror and asked, 'Who won the fashion show?'

'I did.'

'That's right. So, who is officially the most handsome boy?'

'I am,' I replied with a broad grin.

We both shouted thrice in our chirpy voices, 'Vasu is the most handsome boy!'

Suddenly, Kavya went silent. I turned to look at her and noticed that her eyes had welled up.

'Why are you crying?'

'Nothing.' She hugged me and mumbled, 'Remember, being dark is also being beautiful!'

3

The Magic of Attraction

My dad owned a small travel company called Meena International Tours. He had purposely added 'International' to the name as we were mostly dealing with foreign customers. Our company operated majorly in Delhi, Jaipur and Agra. About forty percent of the first-time tourists planned the Golden Triangle tour to explore the various aspects of the Indian landscape. Dad had five Toyota Innovas and two Tata Indica cars.

I had very little understanding of his business, but I still loved visiting the airport. Perhaps because of my fascination for airplanes. I often accompanied dad to welcome foreign guests by holding the placard with their names. I made sure to greet them with a glowing smile, which they deeply appreciated.

I think the same smile had worked its magic on my classmates as well. After the fashion show, a few people had started talking to me in class, but I continued to sit on the last bench. Radhika was getting more attention than ever before. Boys started offering her their notes, lunch boxes and the seats next to them.

The class also invented new nicknames for me – "The vampire", "the dark man" and "a lucky dog", but at least nobody laughed at me anymore.

•

The most awaited day for any child is his or her birthday. It is a special day and even the school lets them wear the clothes of their choice to school. They get pampered with so many tasty delicacies at home and teachers are also more lenient with them.

On my birthday too, the fridge was full of my favourite goodies – Mango Bite toffee, Uncle Chipps, Rasna and one large bottle of cold drink. Mom handed over a bundle of mango candies to me. Thinking that no one was watching me, I went to the corner and opened the packet to keep a few candies in my pocket.

'Why are you stuffing these in your pocket?' mom asked, startling me.

'I am taking some for myself,' I said and gazed down, red-faced.

She smiled and handed another bundle of mango candies to me. 'No need to hide them, Vasu. There's one more packet in the fridge. You can distribute these in the class.'

Kavya gave me a bizarre look. She almost burst into flames when mom gave me a fifty-rupee note. I flagged the paper currency in front of her face to add fuel to her anger.

As I reached my class, Ms Vidya called me to the front of the class and told everyone to sing the birthday song for me. I was beaming with excitement throughout the show. I gave two candies to Vidya ma'am. She stroked my head as a gesture to give her blessings.

'Do you wish to distribute the candies to other teachers?' Vidya ma'am asked me. I nodded eagerly.

'Very well! You can also pick your best friend along with you.'

I did not know why I needed company to distribute candies on my birthday. I looked at all the familiar faces – Pankaj, Mahesh, Nikita, two Nehas and the rest of the class. Everyone wanted to miss the class and come with me. Then I looked at Radhika and kept gazing at her.

'Who is your best friend, Vasu?'

'Radhika!' I answered with a smile on my face.

There was a loud gasp that echoed in the class. Almost immediately, Pankaj made a comment, 'Black and white are still trending.' I heard his remark, but Vidya ma'am didn't.

Radhika and I walked out of the class, sporting smiles. We distributed the candies in the staff room, including the cultural secretary, PT teacher and lab assistants. Radhika started counting the leftover candies.

'You want to have some more candies?' I asked.

She did not say anything, but I extended my bag towards her. 'Please take more.'

She picked one.

'You can take more,' I said with a pleasant smile.

'Really? Thanks.'

She dug out about six-seven candies from the packet, but wasn't able to hold them in her tiny hands. She came close to me and nudged my shoulder. For the first time, I saw her up close. Her face was bright and radiant. She was fair, but that day, she seemed a little pinkish as well.

'You are my best friend,' she said and nudged my shoulder again. A strange yet exhilarating sensation ran through me.

'Why are you so silent, Vasu?'

'I want to ask you something, Radhika.' She arched her eyebrows and looked so pretty. 'Which fairness cream do you use?'

'Excuse me! I don't use any cream.'

'But this is definitely not your natural colour?'

'This *is* my real skin tone,' she said, getting a bit irritated.

'So, is your mom also fair?'

'Yes, but mom uses Vicco Turmeric.'

•

My mom always said that we are all beautiful, irrespective of our skin colour. But somehow, after seeing Radhika, a couple of questions settled in my head. Mom always instructed Kavya to wash her face regularly, use a face pack and avoid going out in the sun. So I knew that only one person could guide me more on this subject. She was lying on her king-size bed like a queen.

'Do you want candies, Kavya?'

She shifted her gaze at me and said, 'What do you need from me?'

I wondered how she had guessed that. She always had an answer to every question I had. If dad would ask for advice on some destination for the family tour, she would be the first one to come up with a name. Mom always asked her advice while shopping. She often helped dad in drafting the letters. I wondered why no one asked for my opinion about anything. Rather, everyone imposed instructions on me.

'Which fairness cream do you use?'

'I don't use anything.'

I ran to Kavya's shelf and pulled out a box which she had been keeping hidden from me. In it, I found a couple of thick white cloth-like things, which felt like an oddly-shaped handkerchief.

'Don't touch my stuff!' she screamed.

'Actually, I am looking for something,' I said, holding the thick cotton handkerchief in my hand. 'What is this?'

'Keep it back!' She roared, as if I was holding an atom bomb.

'What is wrong with you?' I yelled back, annoyed at her screams.

'You are sneaking into my personal space.'

'I just wanted to know which fairness cream you use.'

She gave me a tube of Fair & Lovely cream. I stared at it. 'Why is our colour not normal, Kavya?'

'We *are* normal. What is the matter, Vasu?'

'Radhika is so fair and beautiful. I want to be like her.'

'You are also a very handsome boy, Vasu. Why do you want to be like someone else?'

'Because I like her complexion more than mine.'

'Do you like her because of her fair skin?'

'I don't know.' I was puzzled at this question.

After a brief pause, Kavya took a long breath. She put her hands on her hips and said, 'Come and sit here!'

I silently sat next to her on the bed. She opened the side table and pulled out a pen and paper. 'Look at this page.'

She doodled something. It seemed like she was making two female figures. She pointed to the left figure and said, 'This is mom, and the second one is Radhika.'

'Who do you like the most among these two?' I put my index figure on mom.

Then she wrote "dark skin tone" over mom's illustration and "fair skin tone" over the other one.

'You love mom irrespective of the skin tone.'

'So?' I asked, confused.

'Vicco Turmeric or Fair & Lovely don't determine the affection you have for your loved ones. There is a compelling force which is much stronger than these superficial aspects.'

'What is that?'

'If a good-looking face was the definition of beauty, then no one would have loved their ageing parents.'

I rubbed my face and took a long breath. 'Then why do I like her?'

She laughed aloud and said, 'Because you are attracted to her.'

I was perplexed by her explanation. Sensing my confusion, she elaborated, 'Attraction is when we are intrigued by someone. We gravitate towards them so much that we want to establish a strong and lasting bond with them.'

After our heartwarming conversation, Kavya slept soundly, while I lay awake for a long time. Sleep evaded me as reality was much more enchanting. I went to the living room where dad was watching a cricket match and praising Sourav Ganguly.

'What happened, Vasu?'

'Nothing, I'm unable to sleep.'

'Why? What is the issue?' he asked, still looking at the TV.

'I guess I am attracted to Radhika.'

Dad's attention quickly diverted towards me. He looked at me with his mouth open. His eyes were almost popping out of his glasses.

'How do you know that?'

'Kavya told me.'

'Kavya...' He said in a low tone. 'Don't worry, attraction is a normal thing.'

'Do you also get attracted to someone?'

Suddenly there was a commotion on the TV screen.

He clenched his jaw and slowly shifted his focus on the TV. Sourav Ganguly got bowled out and papa yelled, 'No Dada no!' Then, he switched off the TV and threw the remote on the sofa.

The next morning, dad delivered the longest one-sided speech to Kavya.

4

Future Goals

I had just started walking towards home from school when I noticed a familiar face walking in front of me. I called out her name. Radhika turned back and stopped walking. She held her hand on the hips and glared at me. 'Why are you chasing me, Vasu?'

'I am not chasing you!'

'I see you coming behind me every day.'

'I'm going home.'

'Where do you live?'

'Mansarover Colony, Varun Path.'

'Which block in Varun Path?'

'D-9.'

'Wow! We stay in the same locality. Why are you walking behind me then? We can walk together.'

I smiled with my glorious white teeth.

'But I have never seen you in the morning?' she asked.

'I usually go with my sister in the morning, but she stays in school till late in the evening, so I return alone.'

She nudged on my shoulder and said, 'Dude, you are not alone.'

Dude! Wow no one ever addressed me dude before.

Radhika talked about the new gift shop and ice-cream joint that had opened near our locality. Later, she took me to her house where I met her mom for the first time. She lived in a two-storey house, which was almost half in size to mine. After a brief interaction, I set out towards my home. For the first time, I felt proud of our big, well-decorated house.

The next day in class, an entire sea of boys had offered a seat to Radhika, but she walked to the end and sat with me on the last bench. A few boys made some rude comments, which I ignored. Radhika was everyone's favourite and I was thrilled to be her friend.

Even though Radhika and I had different personalities, our academic performance was nearly the same. We were mediocre students who struggled to memorise the vast syllabus. While I tried hard to push my limits to excel, Radhika gave up easily. She had no interest in books and would often get distracted during class. Gradually, Radhika and I had planted ourselves permanently on the last bench.

It was a cold day and our maths teacher had just finished his lecture. There was a deafening silence after his departure. Radhika swallowed hard by looking at her notes and closed the notebook abruptly.

'Maths sucks!'

I nodded. Then I realized that in my case, not only maths but almost all subjects were the same.

'Are you worried only about maths?' I asked.

'I guess I am worried about the entire education system.'

We had not even recovered from the torture of maths when Ms Malini entered the class. Her presence was always followed by a deadly silence. She was one of those rare teachers who came straight to the back benchers while teaching.

Ms Malini walked towards us and looked at Radhika, as if asking, 'Why are you sitting with this moron?' Fortunately, she did not say anything.

After a brief silence, she shouted.

'Students, today in the moral science class, we are going to discuss how to have an aim in life. Basically, you have to ponder on this question "Where do you want to be in fifteen years?" Everyone must share their ambitions and goals with us. Please note that it should be practical and achievable.'

I looked at Radhika and told myself, 'Even after fifteen years, I want to be in the same class, sitting on the back bench with her.'

'Any doubt?' Ms Malini asked.

A student raised his hand and she permitted him to speak.

'Ma'am, what if we don't have anything in mind?'

'Shut up and sit down. Think more and figure it out. If you don't have a clear purpose, you will be lost in the future. If you want more ideas and clarity, you can discuss with your seat partners.'

Radhika glanced at me and asked, 'What do you want to do in fifteen years?'

'I don't know,' I replied with a confused look.

'Okay! Let me help you. What do you like to do the most?'

'I like welcoming the guests that my dad goes to receive at the airport. I love interacting with them to know their unique stories and tell them about our beautiful heritage.'

'Really?'

'Yes.'

She thought for a couple of seconds and said, 'You can say that you want to become a tour guide.'

'Wow!' I liked the idea. 'What about you?' I asked her.

She blushed a little and said, 'I want to marry a rich man.'

This was the first time she had mentioned the word 'marriage'. My heart started beating rapidly.

'Why do you want to marry a rich guy?'

'A big car, fancy house, a lavish life and no work!'

'Time's up!' Ms Malini burst the imaginary bubble we were in. 'Please share your thoughts on where you see yourself in the future.'

I heard a doctor, an engineer, a scientist, a teacher, an athlete, an actor, model, and most of them wanted to open their own business. I never thought there were so many options in life.

Finally, my turn had come and I said, 'I want to become a tour guide and learn about different cultures.'

Ms Malini looked at me and said, 'Hmm, achievable goal.' And few had giggled for no reason.

•

I was sitting on the sofa and my dad was glued to a news channel on TV.

'Seems like Vasundhara Raje will win the Jaipur state elections.' I did not understand what he was talking about and wondered why he was so engrossed in the news. Suddenly his phone rang. After a brief conversation, he said in an agitated voice, 'Daniel also ran away! He was one of our most popular tour guides.'

Out of curiosity, I asked, 'What educational qualification do you need to become a tour guide, dad?'

'Nothing specific, but it is helpful if you learn a foreign language - German, Russian or English.'

'So many languages?'

He flared his nostril and said, 'You need to top in every exam for that.'

I never thought a tour guide was so educated.

'Can I come with you to receive the German guest tomorrow?'

'It's Sunday, so I guess you can come, Vasu!'

I returned to the room and found Kavya laughing at me. I threw a pillow on her face.

'Why do you want to become a tour guide?' she finally uttered amidst laughter.

'Radhika gave me this suggestion. Besides, I like meeting new people.'

'Seems like you are listening to her *a lot* these days.' She winked at me.

I rolled my eyes at her and asked, 'Kavya, I need your advice!'

'No advice until you call me didi.'

'Kavya...... *didi*, please help.'

'Yes. Tell me what the problem is?'

'Are we a rich family or poor?'

'It depends.'

I frowned. I hated her answer. She never replied to me in simple words.

'Could you please explain, Kavya ... didi?'

'See, we are the richest in some ways.'

'How?' I asked excitedly.

'Suppose we have a big house. What will you do?'

'I will sleep on a big bed.'

'You already have a big bed, and it is bigger than you.' I looked at her king-size bed and my jaw fell.

'What about a car?' she checked.

'We have five Innova cars and two Tata Indica cars.'

'These are taxis.'

'But they are cars.'

'So, we are rich?'

'Basically, it depends on what you want.'

I recollected that papa gave me money whenever I needed it. Mom always made the dishes of our choice. Twice in a year, we went for family vacation. And, we had so many cars.

A radiant smile appeared on my face.

'What happened, Vasu?'

I stood up on her bed and shouted, 'I am the richest man.'

Kavya pulled me down and shouted, 'Go, jump to your bed. This is my bed, my property.'

5
A Kind Heart

Kavya Speaks

Hi, I am Kavya, Vasu's elder sister. I thought I'd have a chat with you and reveal a different side of Vasu's personality.

He had a weird reason to write this book, but it would not be complete without my intercession. Everyone in our family has a dark complexion. It seemed god loved to paint us all in the same colour. Vasu is no different. He has a magnificent smile which brings out the purity and innocence of his heart. The best thing about him is that he is always eager to spread happiness in the lives of the people around him. His simplicity may be perceived as his weakness, but I have been teaching him to harness the power of his inner goodness to embrace his personality.

Initially, Vasu struggled with his studies as he could not remember addresses or complex chemical formulas and theorems. We thought he was just lazing around, but gradually, my parents noticed some unusual behavioural patterns. Like this one instance when we were watching our favourite cartoon Mowgli. I was laughing heartily but Vasu was staring listlessly at the screen.

Even while growing up, I noticed he did not display his emotions uninhibitedly. Though, he loved being pampered with warm hugs. My parents consulted a child psychologist when he was seven, who informed us that Vasu was a slow learner, in comparison to others his age.

When the doctor saw my parents' confused expression, he explained, 'He has been slow in achieving his life milestones like sharing his expressions, feelings and also articulating his own thoughts to you. Moreover, if a child scores an IQ between 70 to 89, we consider him to be a slow learner. This range of IQ is considered as a borderline for low average intellectual capability.

'Dad itched his head, and mom flared her nostrils. So, the doctor tried explaining it in a more unsophisticated manner. The child might be physically in class fifth but intellectually he would belong to class third.'

'So, if we make him repeat two years in the same class, will he be able to catch up with other students?' mom asked.

The doctor shrugged in helplessness and said, 'This is not going to help! The challenge of being a slow learner is that he will not qualify for any special services, special education or even a helpful individualized educational plan (IEP).'

'Then how will he become a fast learner?' my mom asked.

'With time, he will learn and become better.'

'What if that does not happen?' my dad asked in an unsettling voice.

There was silence in the room and the doctor was wondering what to say. After a brief pause, he said, 'Well! There is nothing wrong in just being a good and kind-hearted person.'

'That's alright. But with time, other kids will become smarter and Vasu will be left behind.'

'You begin to lose the battle when you start comparing your milestones with others,' the doctor said.

He summed everything in one line. At that very moment, we realized that Vasu was an average looking boy, with below-average intelligence quotient.

6

The Ideal King

Five years later

Life went on smoothly, and we had passed the class tenth board examination with great difficulty. I secured close to 52% and Radhika had barely managed a few marks more than me.

I was disheartened as I knew that I could have performed better. While walking back home, I was thinking about how papa would react to my marks. He would certainly be disappointed. Mom would never allow me to have ice-cream anymore and Kavya would tease me.

When I reached home, papa was smiling at me. He called me and asked lovingly, 'What gift do you want?'

I was intrigued to see his reaction.

Mom suggested, 'Let's have dinner outside.'

I went silently to my room and Kavya shouted, 'You have performed so well. I am really proud of you!' She gave me a warm hug and all my apprehensions drifted away.

•

Radhika and I opted for Humanities stream for further studies, since the cut-off for Science and Commerce was beyond 60%. It was quite common for students with high marks to opt for science, and average students to pick commerce.

Kavya, in the meantime, had finished her BCA and was struggling with her job and higher education. The society had drilled in the belief that there were only two courses that could guarantee a successful life – engineering and medicine. And if you studied humanities, you would either become a teacher or remain unemployed. I did not think that way, and the lack of options was the best thing for me. I could be anyone I wanted to be.

In terms of vocational opportunities, Jaipur offered a variety of computer and certificate course. Kavya joined a one-year course with Aptech Computers to hone her technical skill.

While on the nation front, Vasundhara Raje, was chosen as the new CM of Rajasthan. BJP had lost the general elections and Atal Bihari Vajpayee had stepped down from the government, making Manmohan Singh, the new prime minister.

He was being mocked as the silent speaker. Many felt that he was "very humane" but not a "well-versed politician". However, I personally liked him. I wish I could meet him and say, 'I could relate to you sir.'

It was the beginning of class eleven. It was one of the special years as we had to participate in all the extracurricular activities since class twelve was busy studying for the final board exams. It was like the last year of enjoyment in our student life. The cultural festival was about to begin and our section had to perform a comic play. Our class teacher Chauhan sir announced, 'Students, we have to perform a stellar play. It would be the most hilarious play that has ever been performed on our stage. We have to win this competition and I have the perfect script for that.'

After giving that energetic speech, Chauhan sir looked at me.

I took the sheets from him and read out the script in an expressive voice. 'There was a beautiful queen who was cursed for the deeds of her previous birth. The curse transformed her into an ugly being at night. But then, a strong king came and liberated her from the curse.'

Chauhan sir looked at the class and added, 'Please note, the play is scheduled for the coming Saturday. We have three full days to practice. So, you may need to skip classes.'

There was an upsurge of excitement in the class. Radhika passed a grin while looking at me.

I heard a few whispers that revealed that the script was not unique. I had watched a similar animated movie last year.

As per our great philosopher Chauhan sir, if you steal from one author, it's plagiarism, but if you borrow from the universe, it's research.

'How many of you are interested to audition for the role of the queen?' he asked.

Namita and Radhika raised their hands. Chauhan sir observed both of them for a few minutes. Then, he kept on looking at Namita for a few seconds and she slowly dropped her hands. It seemed she understood that she was not cut out for the role. Now the most beautiful girl was crowned as the queen for the play without any opponent.

'Who wants to be the king?' Chauhan sir asked vivaciously. His face beamed as if he was going to give away the reign of the city. There were nine pairs of hands in the air. After seeing Radhika as the queen, I raised my hand confidently.

'Seems like we are going to have a tough competition for the role of the king.'

He walked to the aisle and was about to pick Gautam. But then, a few students objected and there was much chaos. 'No sir, this is unfair.'

'Okay! Let's have an audition.' He wrote a few lines and announced that the student who would deliver these lines with impeccable confidence and flair would win the part. The dialogues were as follows:

Hey, brave queen! I am not only a husband, but a king too. I am here to fight for the glory of our kingdom. I am not sure if I would return alive, but if I die on the battlefield, please marry my younger brother.

My eyes widened after hearing the dialogues. I started enacting the part in my mind again and again. Chauhan sir called the contenders one by one. The classroom had become the backstage of a dramatic society.

Finally, my turn came. I walked to the centre and a few guys whispered, 'The real king has come up to save his queen.'

Before I recited the lines, I took a minute to modulate my voice. I needed some motivation so I asked Chauhan sir, 'Can I deliver the dialogues by looking at the queen?'

'Which queen?' he asked surprised.

'I meant Radhika, sir. I will be able to express the feelings better.'

The entire glass squealed and hooted. Chauhan sir passed an awkward smile and said, 'Okay, no problem!'

I looked at Radhika and an unknown creative inspiration engulfed me. Taking a deep breath, I spoke the dialogues with a lot of emotion and drama. While enacting the part, I slipped into the shoes of the king to experience his agony so that I could capture it in my performance.

After I completed my dialogues, some students clapped, including Radhika. Slowly, there was a domino effect, and the whole class clapped in unison. This gave me immense confidence to believe that I could be the king of my queen.

Chauhan sir saw the class's response and went outside, saying that he would need some time to decide the winner.

'Wow, you are a hidden champ,' Radhika said, making me blush.

It was a rare moment when a sheep roared like a tiger. An introvert boy like me had pushed his limits and excelled.

After some time, Chauhan sir walked back in and declared, 'I have decided that the role of the king will go to a good-looking boy who acts well. After all, a king should *look* like a king!'

'Why are looks important when the decision should be made on the basis of acting skills?' Gaurav asked.

'Because a beautiful queen would only marry a handsome king.'

Chauhan sir looked at me and a wave of sympathy ran on his face. Looking away from me, he said, 'The role of the king will be played by Pankaj.'

The class cheered and Radhika gazed at me. She stood from her seat suddenly and said, 'This is not fair, sir.'

'Radhika, there are other roles where we need talented actors, like *sainik, senapati, pujari*. Everyone cannot be the king.'

The bell rang and Chauhan sir left the classroom. Pankaj was gloating and my cheeks looked bloated with fury.

Radhika shouted at Pankaj, 'Stop this nonsense. This is really unfair!'

'Why unfair? The king has to be smart and good-looking.'

'Why does he have to be smart and good-looking?'

'Haven't you seen how the characters of heroes like king Ram, Tipu Sultan, Prithvi Raj Chauhan and Akbar are shown in movies? They are always played by attractive men. All the heroes are handsome, and villains are ugly.' He finished off, giving me a sideways glance.

'Seems like only *you* are watching those nonsense TV shows,' Radhika replied.

'Haven't you read comics book? Nagraj, Dhruv and Doga, or take any superhero like Spiderman or Batman. They are all smart and handsome.'

'This is all bullshit.'

'Now, I am the king. And this bull will not shit.'

Radhika was about to explode but I held her hand. Deep down, I felt as if another king was trying to conquer the heart of my queen.

•

We were soon to have a mid-term break for Navratri. It's a festival for all of us to rejoice with family, so dad and mom were getting ready to go to Udaipur to our uncle's house for the celebrations. Kavya and I were supposed to stay back since the school break was still a couple of days away.

'What happened, Vasu? Why do you look so upset?' Kavya asked, reading my mind.

'Nothing!' My spirits were dampened so I asked dad, 'Can I join you two?'

'You don't want to participate in the cultural programme?' Kavya asked before dad could breathe a word.

I looked at her with a dejected expression. My fallen face must have answered her question as she did not continue the conversation.

'Kavya, you can also come with us. What will you do alone at home?' dad suggested.

Kavya rolled her eyes and took a long breath. She knew she had no choice.

The very next day, we left for Udaipur. My uncle was delighted to see the entire family. He took pride in flaunting his mansion. It was almost double the size of our house. They even had a temple inside.

A grand *puja* ceremony was organized in the in-house temple. Everyone assembled for the *aarti*. I looked at the sculptures of lord Vishnu, lord Rama, and Maa Durga. Suddenly, Pankaj's words came rushing to my mind.

I got up from my seat and silently walked out of the room. It could have gone unnoticed by the entire world, but not by Kavya.

Later that night, Kavya asked me. 'What happened, Vasu? Why did you leave in the middle of the puja?'

'I don't feel like talking to anyone.' I took a deep breath, gritted my teeth and let the breath out. I was trying to control my emotions, but failing miserably at it.

Kavya came closer to me. She put her hand over my head affectionately and said, 'You can talk to me, Vasu. Remember, we are best friends!'

'Why are all the gods and goddesses so good-looking? And the asuras so unattractive?'

'Who said that, Vasu?'

'That is not important. Why are all heroes so fair and the villains so dark?'

'What about lord Krishna?' Kavya posed a counter-question.

'He is also a good-looking god!' I pointed out.

'It does not matter how gods look, Vasu. We worship them for their intrinsic qualities, not their external appearance. Lord Rama is worshipped because he demonstrates the traits of an ideal person. Hanuman ji is revered because he is the epitome of loyalty and commitment. We should take inspiration from their actions, not their looks.'

Looking at my morose expression, she dragged me into the temple and showed me the statue of goddess Kali.

"Look at her, Vasu! Goddess Kali may not be fair, but she embodies incredible strength and courage. Your complexion does not matter. Your character will determine the kind of person you want to be!

'Sometimes I feel I am inferior,' I said in a dejected voice.

'But why? It is natural! Plus, these are all superficial features. Inside, we are all the same.'

I had almost yawned after hearing her sleep-inducing, stale monologue. I looked at the statue of goddess Kali. I wanted to believe Kavya, but something did not feel right.

'But I was rejected because I was not handsome enough to play the role of the king, Kavya.' I narrated the audition story and how Chauhan sir had chosen Pankaj over me.

Kavya was stunned. She flared her nostrils and tried to divert my attention.

'Do you like Radhika?' That did the trick.

'Yes.'

'Do you love Radhika?'

'I don't know. I just wanted to be her king.'

Kavya chuckled.

'Why are you laughing at me, Kavya?'

'You are worried about getting the attention of one Radha when you can charm many gopis.'

I shrugged in disbelief. Her comparison made no sense to me.

'You are Vasu. Don't you know that? Vasu was the name of lord Krishna.'

'So?'

'Krishna is also dark-complexioned and yet, we worship him for his simplicity and intelligence. You are our Krishna.'

'But he is a god, Kavya.'

'No, he is the incarnation of god. You know how many gopis admired him and believed him to be their partner? Sixteen thousand!'

'Really?'

'Yes.'

I tried to envision the charming Krishna, surrounded by many girls. How could he remember the names of all the sixteen thousand gopis? How would he even recognize them? But the glorious image did not last for too long. Dressed in the lavish queen's costume, Radhika invaded my mind. She was standing next to her king, Pankaj. I started losing my cool again.

'Lord Krishna may have many gopis by his side, but I need my Radhika only.'

'Oh, lover boy!' I flushed as Kavya ruffled my hair.

7
The Underdog

We returned to Jaipur in two days. I wanted to avoid the cultural fest, so I pretended to be unwell. Mom and dad believed me, but Kavya was sceptical.

'Why are you not going to school, Vasu?'

'I'm not feeling well.'

'As if I will believe you! Out with the truth, now!' She glared at me.

'I don't want to see Radhika becoming someone else's queen.'

'Is that the *only* reason?'

I turned my face away from her. Kavya put her thick computer book on the bed and went silent for a few seconds. It was the most dangerous time for me. She got up and closed the door of our room. I was surprised by her sudden excitement.

'This is a great opportunity, Vasu!'

The word "opportunity" offered some solace to my grief-stricken heart.

'When you have lost hope, you have lost everything. But life works in mysterious ways. It will give you a hint during desperate times. You should be smart enough to notice it.'

After delivering her speech, she stopped blinking. Suddenly she looked like a devi who appears every morning on Aastha channel. I was unable to make sense of her.

'Let us play the underdog strategy, Vasu.'

'What is the underdog strategy?'

'An underdog is a person who is expected to lose. You should go to school with a dull face. By seeing your dampened spirits, she will sympathize with you. Sympathy is the first sign of affection.'

'But it would be hard to see her becoming someone else's queen.'

'You just go, lover boy! If it gets unbearable, then you can skip the performance.'

'If I skip her performance, then what is the use of going to school?'

'She needs your best wishes before the play.'

I stood back on my feet and flashed a victorious smile. I loved Kavya's strategy of transforming this rejection into an opportunity.

'I will give her my best wishes and she will give me...'

'Sympathy!' We shouted in unison.

•

The school was tastefully decorated with colourful posters. The walls displayed catchy slogans which could inspire anyone. A huge speaker was playing a pleasant song, adding to the exuberance of the environment.

I found most of the classes to be empty and the benches pushed back along the corners. I spotted a few beautifully dressed girls and smiling boys. I sighed and walked silently towards my class. I could see only those students who never participated in any extracurricular activities. Basically, they were married to books. I looked at them and it seemed that they were silently regretting the fact that they did not participate in any cultural programme.

I took out my tiffin and thought of finishing it. I was not irritated, but I guess I had nothing to do. Chauhan sir came running to the class. He was more excited than the students. 'What are you doing here?'

'Studying, sir!' Sunita said, adjusting her thick spectacles.

'Please assemble in the auditorium. The event is about to start.'

'Sir, can we study in the class?' I asked.

'Everyone must be there in the hall and attendance will be taken.'

'Attendance?'

'Yes. Ours will be the first play. So, hurry up!

I grumbled as I would not be able to leave the hall immediately as I had hoped for. I wished that I could kill Kavya. I stopped eating my lunch and packed my bag. Suddenly, Sunita came near me and said, 'It happens Vasu.'

I was surprised to receive Sunita's sympathy. Perhaps, Kavya's strategy was working.

We all sat at a commonplace in the auditorium so that Chauhan sir could easily take our attendance. I was engulfed by the feelings of rejection and despair. Unable to control my emotions, I closed my eyes. I felt that someone had taken a seat next to me, but I didn't open my eyes. I wished I could vanish into thin air.

Chauhan sir started calling out the names of the students to mark our attendance. After taking few names in his mundane voice, he shouted my favourite, 'Radhika...'

A voice said, 'Present sir!'

Her voice was music to my ears. I opened my eyes and saw Radhika sitting next to me.

'You did not participate in the play?'

'Where did you go, Vasu?'

'I went to Udaipur.'

'You could have informed me.'

'Why? What happened?'

'You went so abruptly just after the audition. I got worried for you. I even went to your house, but there was no one.'

'You came to my house?'

'Yes.'

If I had a tail, I would have certainly started wagging it in the air.

'But what happened to your play? Why are you sitting here?'

'I withdrew my name.'

'Why?'

'How can I become the queen if you are not the king!'

My heart was filled with immense happiness. Perhaps the underdog strategy had worked.

8

Friend-zoned

Whenever I read through Kavya's computer books, I would come across some strange terms like LAN, VAN, Java, Pascal and other such things. If the names are so tedious, I didn't want to imagine how complicated their meanings would be. I realized that computer science was not my cup of tea.

My twelfth grade examinations were about to end now. While I was still coping with the pressure of studying, my dad had initiated the dreaded topic, 'Where will Vasu go for his college studies?'

Unable to think of a convincing answer, I raised my eyebrows.

Mom said, 'Let him finish the exams first.' She understood my apprehensions, but who could stop Kavya.

'Vasu will join a hotel management course,' she declared.

'Why?' I asked, shocked by her sudden revelation.

'Because you wanted to get into the hospitality industry. And you can also help dad in his business then!' she said matter-of-factly.

'Dad is not into hotels.' I was about to initiate a battle for my freedom, but I guess my struggle ended even before it began as dad beamed at Kavya's idea.

'Good suggestion, Kavya!'

•

It was my last day at school and I had my history exam. I was feeling miserable since a significant phase of our lives was coming to an end. It would be my last chance to see Radhika in school uniform.

After the exam, Radhika and I headed towards home. I walked at a snail's pace with drooping shoulders. She nudged me and asked, 'What's up?'

I stared at her with a blank expression. Then, I diverted my eyes towards the road ahead to reach my destination.

We crossed an ice cream parlour on our way. 'Let's have ice cream!' Radhika halted in front of the parlour.

I was not willing to eat anything, but I nodded anyway. She ordered two strawberry-flavoured ice creams and handed one to me. As she took the first bite, her cheeks glowed with joy. She looked like a cute pink doll. The slurping sound which she produced with every lick of the gelato was adorable. I tried hard to make the sweet ice cream cover the bitter truth that this moment could be my last time with her.

'What happened? You look so sad, Vasu.'

'Tomorrow onwards, there would be no school.'

'Yes. But we would venture into college,' Radhika said, looking happy and seemingly excited for the start of the new chapter.

'So, which course do you plan to join?' I asked.

'I have already applied for B.Sc. in Computer Science from the University of Rajasthan.'

'Oh! You have already applied?'

'Yes! What about you?'

'I will probably join some hotel management course.'

'Good for you,' Radhika said and continued licking the frozen dessert.

Meanwhile, the ice cream in my hand had already started melting. I took a large bite, as if savouring a samosa. I wanted to ask Radhika how I could meet her again.

'It's such a good feeling. Isn't it?' Radhika said, relishing her ice cream.

'What is good here?'

'Ice cream.'

Once we finished our ice creams, I walked silently while she continued to talk about her favourite flavour and other ice cream shops. When we reached her place, I wanted to hug her, but was scared.

'I am going to miss you, Radhika.'

'Aww, you are such a cute baby.'

'I am an eighteen-year-old boy, not a baby.' She laughed.

'But tell me, how will we meet again?'

'We stay in the same locality. You can come to my house anytime.'

'I hope you parents don't mind if I come to meet you sometimes.'

She thought for a few seconds and said, 'You can come with Kavya then.'

Before stepping towards her house, I squinted my eyes and asked, 'So I can come to your house with a girl?'

She shrugged and shook her head in exasperation. We realized that we had almost reached our complex.

Radhika stopped before me. She stared into my eyes and said, 'You are so sweet, Vasu. You will always be my best friend.'

•

I got admission in the Indian Institute of Hotel Management in Jaipur. My college was supposed to start in a month so I had plenty of time to kill. I was living life king-size – I woke up late and did not even shave on most days. Sony TV was on a marathon of airing the movie *Sooryavansham* and the English channels were running James Bond movies repeatedly. I spent most of my time binge watching series and latest movies. The world seemed confined to me.

I crossed Radhika's house once every day, just to catch a glimpse of her. I met her mom twice and offered a respectable *namaste*. We met each other a few times during the parent-teacher meetings.

Residing in the same locality, our families were also familiar with each other.

I lost interest in sports. My song preference changed from pop to romantic, and got stuck on sad ones. I wasted most of my time binge-watching series and movies.

It was a dry season for dad's business. Jaipur is a semi-desert region, which has three distinct seasons. Winter is the best and the only suitable season to visit the city. Since dad had some time at hand, he planned a family trip to Mount Abu. But Kavya could not go on the trip as she had some essential official work. I stayed back with her.

The absence of our parents gave both of us some freedom. No one was there to force us to wake up early. Kavya could now watch her favourite channels. There was no one to supervise us, so we enjoyed these moments to the fullest.

I was lying on Kavya's bed, cluelessly looking at the fan dancing overhead.

'Oye, why are you lying on my bed?' Kavya asked while entering the room. She was obsessed with her bed, cosmetics, laptop, and mirror. She never wanted to share anything.

I fumed. Why were all the good things given to her? She had the bigger almirah, a large-sized bed, and even a scooty.

It seemed I was treated secondarily. I shifted to my bed on hearing the harsh words from my sister.

'What happened?' Kavya asked.

'Nothing! Why?'

'I asked you to shift to your bed, and you did! No fight, no resistance!'

'You want to fight?'

She rested her back on her bed and I was lying on mine.

'Don't be silent if you have nothing sweet to say. Let's fight.'

I did not reply and turned my face in another direction.

'What happened, lover boy? You look lost in your school memories.'

'No, I am just getting bored.'

'Baby, you are not getting bored.'

'Baby? Don't call me baby.'

'Okay, lover boy, what is the matter?'

'Nothing.' I said, looking at the ceiling fan.

'Looks like someone is missing Radhika,' she said in a singsong voice.

'How do you know that?'

'The way you are roaming around her house daily, anyone can guess.'

'Why am I missing her so much and she is not?'

'How do you know she is *not* missing you?'

I shrugged.

'Do you love her or is it just physical attraction?'

'What is the difference between love and attraction?'

She stood on her bed as lord Krishna stood beside Arjuna in the *Mahabharata* to impart worldly knowledge and wisdom.

'Come here, lover boy,' Kavya said, patting the bed on her side. 'Love emerges from the heart and attraction comes from...' she said and pointed at my crotch.

'What?' I was confused.

'Have you ever kissed her?'

'Kavya, come on!'

'Oh, then what exactly do you feel when you see her?'

'I feel like talking to her.'

'Only talking, Vasu? You never felt like hugging her or getting close to her?'

I shook my head. She opened her mouth and stopped blinking. 'Then why do you even miss her?'

'I already said, I miss talking to her.'

'Do you ever imagine having sex with her?'

'This is nonsense, Kavya!' I was flabbergasted by how our conversation was unfolding.

'Why nonsense? Everyone does that.'

'I have never thought about her in *that* way.'

'Do you ever imagine her in a sexy dress?'

I shook my head.

'Then why are you missing her?'

'I miss talking to her.'

She swallowed hard and took a deep breath. She got up from her bed and started pacing back and forth in the room. She gazed at me twice and smiled. Then she looked at the corner of the room. I was getting restless.

'What happened? What are you thinking?'

'You are in love, my boy.'

I smiled. Perhaps, I was blushing. Who knows!

'Don't pass that stupid smile.'

I made a face.

She took a pen and paper and drew a big line across the centre of the page. On one side, she wrote "Hell" and on the other side, she wrote "Heaven".

Puzzled, I looked at both sides and asked, 'What is this?'

'If she also loves you, then you are in heaven.'

'And if not...?' I asked, out of nervousness.

'Then it's a one-sided love story. That is hell!'

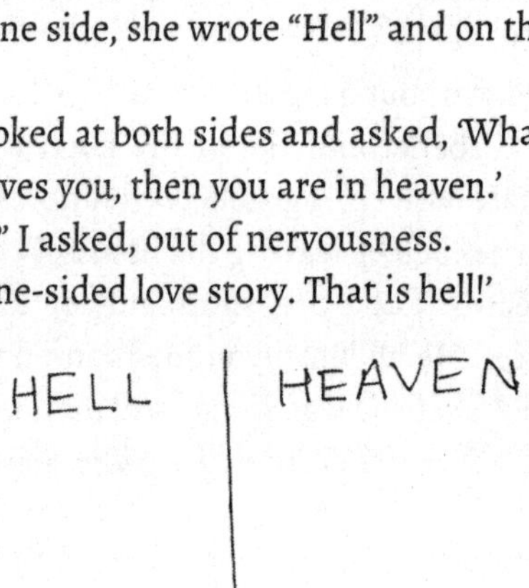

HELL | HEAVEN

I gulped my saliva and demanded an explanation. 'How will I decide whether I am in hell or heaven?'

'When you think all is lost, life gives you a hint. You need to be smart enough to comprehend the hint.'

I thought about Radhika. I joined my palms and gently rubbed them, wondering what clue was hidden here. Kavya was sitting on her bed and I saw her staring at me.

'What is the hint here?' I asked.

She looked at me with sympathetic eyes and said in a low voice, 'I am also wondering about the same.'

I pursed my lips and flared my nostrils,

'I want to be in heaven. I cannot afford to be in hell.'

'Sorry to say this but nothing is coming to my mind.'

'No, didi. Please help me.'

'Stop buttering me by calling me didi.'

'Didi, please.'

'Don't patronize me.'

She went silent. Taking a long, deep breath, she demanded, 'Can I have a cigarette?'

'What! You smoke?'

'I cannot think without a cigarette.'

I gawked in disbelief and flared my nostrils. I was not in a position to negotiate with her. I grabbed a few notes from my drawer and checked with her before leaving the house. 'Which brand?'

'Go to the nearest Kallu pan shop and say Kavya madam has asked for cigarettes. He will give you my brand on his own,' Kavya spoke dramatically, as if she was some local mafia.

I walked out and reached the pan shop. I asked the *panwari*, 'Uncle, one cigarette.'

'You too?'

'No. It is for didi,' I said, my cheeks flaming red with shame.

'Kavya madam?' he stiffened as if he was her secretary.

He pulled a pack of Marlboro Red from the top shelf, along with two small packets of silver coated cardamom seeds.

'This is complementary for Kavya madam.'

I flushed and my breath was heavy. I looked at him for a few seconds without blinking my eyes. I wished I could kill him and his Kavya madam.

I rushed back home and handed over the things to her.

'Make a cup of tea for me!' Kavya ordered.

I shook my head as a sign of an indifferent response, but made tea for her anyway. I even served it with two cookies. Kavya sat on the sofa and rested one leg on the armrest. She took a deep puff and closed her eyes. I was getting restless and she was acting up.

After finishing her tea, she said, 'Please bring a paper and pen.'

My lips curved into a smile. I followed her commands like an obedient student. This time, she drew more lines on the paper.

'Now tell me one thing. Do you know everything about her?' I nodded.

'Yes, almost everything.'

'What is her bra size?'

'It must be 30 I think.'

'A little small.' She mumbled, 'But how did you know that?'

'That's your size as well.'

Kavya rolled her eyes and fidgeted.

'Any hidden secret?'

'She doesn't like her father.'

'Why?'

'He drinks a lot. And when he is high, he fights with her mom.'

'You know about her periods?'

'Yes.'

'She told you?'

'No, we share the same period like history, geography, English.'

Kavya looked at me with an open mouth. Then, she exhaled, gritted her teeth and shook her head in disbelief. She lit another cigarette. I was getting irritated by her expressions and mood swings. She signalled me to the sofa, placed the paper on the table, and made a big circle.

'Hmm, your problem is that you are friend-zoned.'

'What is friend-zoned?'

'Means you are just a friend.'

'But is it really a problem?'

'Actually, it is a solution in a lot of cases. But in your case, it is a problem.'

I held my head. It looked like I was working on some complicated computer program.

Kavya read my confused face and said, 'Listen, Vasu. She likes you as a friend but she does not love you as a boyfriend. I am just trying to understand.'

'What is the difference between a friend and a boyfriend?'

'A friend can share everything, but cannot have...' She paused and said, 'Sex!'

My eyes flickered and I tried to process her words. 'So, she cannot have sex with me?'

'Oh, man! You are such a pervert!'

'I'm not a pervert. You are the one who said this.'

'Our target is to transform this friendship into love.'

'But how?'

'First, you need to arrange a regular meeting with her. We need to figure out something quickly.'

'Why quickly?'

'Oh, my innocent baby! A pretty girl is taking admission in a college far away from home.'

'So what?'

'There are many crocodiles in the pond to impress the beautiful fish.'

9

The First Step

My parents returned from their trip with a box of assorted sweets and lovely memories. Mom showed us the pictures they had clicked at a studio in Mount Abu and asked me to keep the pictures in the family album.

While flipping through the sheets of the album, I saw my picture with Radhika from our Halloween fashion show. She was dressed like a vampire. I traced my fingers over the picture and swallowed hard.

'Don't you dare cry for her!'

I turned around and saw Kavya standing behind me.

'Didi, my situation is like a patient whose diagnosis is complete, but no one has a clue about the treatment.'

She rolled her eyes and clamoured, 'Let's check her profile on Facebook.'

We logged in with my password on Facebook. She looked at Radhika's profile and scrolled down to check her pictures.

'She has posted some new pictures. She looks so beautiful. Let me like them,' I said, while scrolling through her timeline.

'Don't you dare press the like button,' Kavya retorted. 'She should not know that we are looking through her profile.'

Kavya took the laptop from me.

'What are you doing, Kavya? Isn't this known as stalking?'

'Oye, lover boy! This is known as research.'

'What?'

'When boys do it, it is called stalking and when girls do it, it is known as research.'

I flared my nostrils and clenched my jaws.

Kavya scrolled through a few pictures. My favourite face was smiling in front of me. My lips curved into a smile. I was amazed to see that Radhika had received so many comments and likes. I marvelled at how she looked more beautiful on Facebook.

'How come her posts have so many comments?'

'She is a girl, Vasu.'

'No! Pankaj also has so many likes and comments.'

'What is the problem with you?'

'When I post any photo, I hardly get any likes or comments. I have even stopped checking my Facebook account.'

'You might be having a few friends.'

'No one sends me any friend requests.'

'Oh!' Kavya gazed at me. Her eyes were filled with deep empathy. I failed to understand her emotion.

After a few minutes, she finally rested on a random picture and gestured me to see. I looked at the picture where Radhika was smiling in an ivory-coloured top.

'She is looking good na?'

'I am talking about the background, idiot! It seems she often visits a temple.'

Kavya scanned a few more posts and landed on another picture where Radhika was dressed in a yellow salwar-kameez, holding a puja thali. The caption said, *Lord Krishna, #Blessedlife.*

'She seems to be a devotee of Krishna so she must be visiting some nearby temple.'

'Which means I can visit the nearest Krishna temple and meet her.'

'Yay!' We both exclaimed in unison.

Kavya and I decided to search for the temple where Radhika visited so that I could meet her.

To begin our research, she typed on Google: *Temples near me.*

The webpage displayed a few names like Krishna Mandir, Shyam Mandir, Kali temple, Sai temple, and ISKCON temple. All these temples were within a radius of two kilometres from our current location.

Kavya remodified the search and entered: *Krishna temple near me.*

The search result showed ISKCON temple, Shree Radha Krishna temple, Shree Shyam temple and Shree Radha Govind Dev temple.

Kavya was again lost in scrolling through Facebook. She ran her palms over her face. Then, she scratched her head twice and looked at the ceiling fan thrice. She was not going to give up easily.

'But Kavya, why can't I ask Radhika directly?'

'What? You are stalking her. How can you ask her directly?'

'We are doing *research* so I can ask her anything.'

She sighed and said, 'Let's try.'

Kavya dialled Radhika's number, and a female voice answered the call.

'Hello, aunty! I am Kavya. May I speak to Radhika?'

'Radhika, your phone,' her mom called out to her.

'Hello!' I was hearing her voice after two weeks.

'Hey Radhika! Vasu here.'

'Hey Vasu! How are you?'

Her voice seemed more melodious on the phone. Or maybe I was drenched in the vibrant colours of love.

'Radhika, which temple do you visit daily?'

'I go to Shree Shyam temple every Saturday. But why, what happened?'

'Nothing. I just thought I could meet you there.'

'Okay, sure! 'But how did you know that I go to a temple?'

'Actually, your Facebook...'

Kavya disconnected the call.

I frowned and shouted, 'Why did you disconnect the call?'

'Are you an idiot?'

'How can you disconnect the call when we were in the middle of a conversation?'

'Stop this nonsense. You are directly telling her that you were stalking her. This way, you may lose her.'

I gave a sceptical nod. Suddenly, the phone rang again. Radhika called this time.

'Hey, I think the line got disconnected,' Radhika said.

'Yes...there was some network issue,' I replied.

'Tomorrow at 6 p.m. then?'

'Sure!'

I hung up with a winning smile, but Kavya did not reciprocate my joy. Rather, she gave me a cold stare.

'Hey, why are you upset?'

'She called you to the temple, right?'

I nodded, elated.

'Vasu, you just got friend-zoned...again!'

10

The Temple Meeting

I shaved and got dressed in a green t-shirt and a pair of blue denims. I hunted for Kavya's expensive perfume. I sprayed it on my t-shirt, lost in its fragrance. It took a few seconds to regain my composure. I wondered what if Kavya would get to know that I have used her stuff.

Suddenly, Kavya entered the room and passed a genuine smile. She scanned me from head to toe and said, 'Wear a wristwatch.'

I obeyed her. The last time I wore my watch was when I had to go to Kavya's friend's birthday party.

I checked my watch and concluded that I was an hour ahead of the scheduled time.

I looked at Kavya and she winked. 'You are looking handsome, lover boy!'

'Can I go now?'

'Wait!' Kavya opened her almirah to fetch something. She handed me the tube of facial cream and said, 'Apply this.'

I read the label on the tube. It was a fairness cream. I massaged my face with the woman's cream and viewed myself in the mirror. The cosmetic did not filter my dark complexion as its label promised. I again dabbed my face with some extra quantity of the white cream. The mirror gave the same response: *You still look the same.*

'I guess you look dashing even without the cream,' Kavya said.

I smiled and left for the temple. It took me ten minutes to reach there but I couldn't see Radhika anywhere. I glanced at my watch. It was 5:30 p.m.

I did not mind waiting for her. I sat on the temple stairs and prayed to god. I looked at the idol of Krishna standing there gracefully, with a flute in his hands and a radiant smile on his face. The beautiful Radha was standing right next to him.

I turned around, only to see Radhika walking towards me. We partially hugged each other, but she did not seem excited. Rather, she asked in a doleful tone, 'Have you finished the puja?'

'Yes, but I can join you.'

I looked at the statue of Radha and Krishna while Radhika was busy offering her prayers. I began to draw similarities between them and my relationship with Radhika. After all, I was Vasu and she was *my* Radha.

As we walked out towards the open area, I wondered whether Radhika would leave now. Before I could ask her anything, she said, 'Let's have lassi.'

We went to Shyam Lassiwala right outside the temple. The shop had a congested seating space, but the owner welcomed us with a warm smile. We ordered two plain, dry fruit lassis.

'How often do you come here, Vasu?'

'I just came here for you as I was missing you... I mean, our school days.'

As we were talking, an old, fragile man entered the shop. Dressed in tattered clothes, he was begging the owner to give him something to drink as he was very thirsty.

'*Yahan kuch nahi hai, baba!*' The owner sent him away with an air of indifference.

I saw the helpless face of the old man. I was so moved by his desperate state that I got up from my seat and ordered a lassi for him. When it was prepared, I walked up to the man and gave it to him.

He looked at me, his eyes brimming with love and gratitude. He kept a hand on my head and blessed me.

When I came back and took my seat, Radhika said, 'That was really thoughtful. I am glad to have a friend like you!'

My smile was broader than I intended to show. Finally, lord Krishna was showering his blessings on me!

'How is everything at home?' I asked to set the conversation rolling.

She looked down at her hands, fidgeting. I guessed it must be her father.

'Why are you upset, Radhika?'

She tightened her lips and said emotionally, 'It feels really good when someone notices your sadness and enquires about it. Actually, dad drinks and fights with mom all the time.'

'But that is an old story. Nothing new, right?' I asked wearily.

'Yes, but yesterday he was diagnosed with high blood pressure. Now, drinking is risky.'

In an attempt to offer comfort, I said, 'Hmm, I understand. It can be tough, but you are a strong girl.'

'Yes, but now school is also closed, so I am sitting at home most of the time. My mind is totally caught up between my parents.'

'So, you hate your father?'

'No, Vasu. He is my father.'

'Can I help you in any way?'

'You are already helping me by hearing me out.'

I noticed that she hadn't even touched her lassi. 'What happened? You did not like it?'

'Actually, I don't like lassi a lot. I was looking for a place to sit and talk. My college will open in ten days. Then I might have some good news to share.'

'True! But why don't you come to the temple daily? It will help you heal.'

'Yes, I guess I can come here every day till my college starts.'

It was hard to control my happiness. If one day spent with her could make that much difference, I would not mind spending my entire life in this temple.

Finally, it was time to say goodbye. The pain of departure was more intense than the happiness of our meeting. It looked like everything had ended too soon.

When we reached her house, Radhika smiled at me and said, 'See you tomorrow, Vasu.'

I was hoping for a parting hug, but then her mom came out. I greeted her mom with folded hands, to which she smiled warmly.

•

I lay on Kavya's bed and stared at the fan. Everything was moving in slow motion. The magic of romance had captured my heart and soul.

Kavya entered the room and shouted, 'What are you doing on my bed?'

I did not move. My body felt weightless and I continued to look at the fan.

'What happened, lover boy? Why are you so thrilled?'

'When you lose everything, life gives you a hint. And this time, life has revealed the biggest secret to me.'

'And what is it?' Kavya asked, coming closer.

'Do you know the meaning of Radhika?'

'What?'

'Radhika means Radha and Vasu means Krishna. We are made for each other. She is my Radha, and I am her Krishna.'

Kavya's facial expression changed. She slowly sat at the corner of the bed.

'What happened? Why are you so upset?' I asked, perplexed by her unpredictable expression.

She rolled her eyes and sighed. Then she cupped her chin and said softly, 'You know, Krishna never married Radha!'

11

A New Friend

I enrolled in a three-year course in hospitality management. I was introduced to new subjects ranging from general hotel operations to catering. Initially, I enjoyed this new exposure, but gradually I felt pressure building up. Nevertheless, the experience was far better than mugging up history and geography.

The college had a very vibrant environment, yet I felt nostalgic for my school days. I was a backbencher here too, but the difference was that instead of Radhika, Usha was my new neighbour. Everyone formed their own circle of friends. Sitting amongst strangers, it was challenging for me to initiate a conversation, which made me miss Radhika even more.

Kavya had joined ICICI Bank as a data analyst. She was doing well in her professional life. She had even gifted herself a mobile phone. At home, the discussion around Kavya's marriage was in full swing. Sadly, Kavya had turned into a guinea pig, trying out various beauty products to get fair skin. She would experiment with different hidden kitchen hacks, applying curd. lemon juice or gram flour. Obsessed with her skincare routine, she no longer stepped out of home in half sleeves or without hand gloves. I would often see mom mixing herbs and powders for Kavya so that she could get a flawless face.

That day too, mom was busy helping Kavya apply a turmeric face pack, hoping that some miracle would happen. Meanwhile, I was lying on the sofa, thinking about Radhika's abusive father.

When mom had left, Kavya came and sat beside me. 'How are your studies going, lover boy?'

'Good! I really enjoy the classes that help us improve our interpersonal relationships. But I miss Radhika a lot!'

'Don't make her your weakness, Vasu. She should be your strength.'

I lifted my eyes and looked at Kavya. Her unrealistic words did not affect me.

'Come here. Let me show you something,' she said while working on the laptop.

'These are matchmaking requests on the matrimonial sites!'

We want a tall, fair, slim and working girl with no relationships in the past. She must be a non Facebook user.

We want a traditional and beautiful girl. She can wear jeans in the house but while stepping out, she must respect our culture by wearing saree and salwar suit.

We read more than ten matrimony descriptions and everyone had highlighted – a tall, slim, fair and beautiful bride.

'Why does everyone want a tall, fair and slim girl?' I asked.

'Fair girls are perceived to be "beautiful". And besides, most of the boys who put such ads are looking for sex in the name of marriage,' Kavya said in an agitated voice.

I was surprised to hear her remark. 'Why are only fair people considered to be beautiful?'

She said thoughtfully, 'Umm, when we were under the British rule, people looked up to their foreign masters. And since they were relatively fairer, they were perceived to be superior. That's how it became a general perception.'

'But now we are free, right? There are no masters now.'

'We are physically free, but still mentally colonized.'

'Do looks matter so much?'

'Yes, that is why my marriage will take a lot of time, while Radhika will get a lot of good proposals without much effort.'

'But why?'

'She is a fair and good-looking girl.'

'But I will wait for your wedding.'

'Vasu, I am talking about Radhika, not yours.'

'But Radhika will be marrying me, right?'

'Yes,' she hesitated. 'I hope you can understand what I am talking about?'

My mood was now ruined. I had no desire to see those matrimonial profiles, so I got up. Before I walked out of the room, Kavya asked a pertinent question and caught my attention.

'How will you meet Radhika now? Have you thought of something?'

'No, she has started going to her new college.'

'Do you want to meet her daily?'

I sat there with a puppy face and wagged my neck.

'Yesterday I met her when she was going to college. She was waiting for an auto-rickshaw,' Kavya said casually.

'It is sad that she has to go by bus everyday.'

'Stupid you are, Vasu.'

'Why, what happened?' I went and sat near her.

'You seem uninterested.'

'No, sorry didi. I am very much interested. Tell me what happened?'

She smirked as if she had won the battle.

'Yesterday, when we had gone for a movie, I saw Radhika taking an auto from her college gate.'

'Oh, so you went for a movie alone?'

'Are you nuts? I am talking about Radhika, not the movie.'

'I am not getting you?'

'Focus, Vasu! I observed that she had to struggle to commute. The good part is that her college starts a little early than yours.'

'So, should I also go by auto?'

'No, you can drop her off by bike.'

'But I don't have a bike.'

'Yeah, but I have a scooty!'

We both passed a clever smile and I said, 'Love you, didi!'

•

The next morning, I was standing a few metres away from her house, ready with my scooty. I knew I would have to cook up a convincing story to persuade her. Just then, I saw Radhika stepping out of her house. My heart skipped a beat. I decided that I shouldn't hide my feelings anymore.

'Hey Vasu! Why are you here so early in the morning? Isn't this Kavya's scooty?'

'Now it's mine as she is taking the taxi.'

'Where are you going?'

'I am going to college. Come, I will drop you.'

Radhika beamed and said, 'Sure!'

She hopped on the back seat and placed one hand on my shoulder. Her touch was exhilarating. I had never imagined that a scooty ride could be so romantic. I drove at the slowest possible speed, thinking myself to be a knight riding a horse.

'Vasu, isn't your college on the other side from here?'

'Don't worry, I will drop you first and then go there.'

'Do one thing. You can drop me near Raj Mandir. From there, I will take an auto and you can go to your college.'

'If you say so, Radhika. By the way, I am also learning to drive a car. And soon, I will have my cell phone too.'

'That's great Vasu!'

I dropped her at the Raj Mandir auto stand. 'How is college otherwise? Did you make any friends yet?'

'Yes, I did. His name is Sanju.'

'Sanju!' The name resonated in my ears.

'Is he your good friend?'

'Yes! We sit together in the class.'

'So, does he also go for lunch with you?'

'Yes.'

'Does he also participate in plays and other cultural activities with you?'

'We are mostly together in college.'

I imagined Sanju sitting with her in the class. I puffed my cheeks and sighed.

Was I feeling jealous?

'How does he look?'

'What does that mean, Vasu?'

'Does he look like me?'

Radhika smiled and said, 'No one is sweet and innocent like you, Vasu.'

12

The Perfect Gift

I switched on my laptop and checked Radhika's friend list. After scrolling a bit, I landed on a profile named Sanju Singh. I clicked the "About us" section and found that he was also from the same college. I checked his picture. His dark eyes were gazing at me, and his fair, V-shaped face seemed to be challenging me.

I was staring at the screen coldly when Kavya walked in. I fidgeted at her unannounced entry. With her hands on her hips, she shouted, 'What are you doing with my laptop?'

'I'm searching for someone on Facebook.'

She peeped at the screen and said, 'Oh my god! He is so smart. Who is he?'

I was surprised by her reaction. 'He is a boy who is hanging out with Radhika in college every day.'

'Oh god!' Kavya said, her demeanour changing rapidly.

There was deadly silence for a while. It looked like both of us had lost a great battle. I closed the laptop without giving any turn off command. Then, I lay on the bed.

She started biting her nails. After thinking hard for a while, she announced, 'The time has come, lover boy.' She spoke as if she was going to give a *brahmastra* to me.

'Time for what?'

'You need to propose to her.'

'Propose for what?'

'Propose to date you.'

'What if she rejects me?' I sat up.

'Radhika is a beautiful girl and a handsome boy is sitting next to her. It's a dangerous sign.'

I swallowed hard.

'If you don't propose to her now, then someone else might.'

I held my head. I wished I had proposed to her back in class five itself.

'When is her birthday?' Kavya asked.

'In two months.'

'Then, propose to her on her birthday!'

•

It was the time when all the domestic telecom companies such as Airtel, Hutch and Reliance had made incoming calls free, but text messages were costing one rupee per delivery. I was hoping to get a new phone soon as it would help me to communicate with Radhika more effectively.

Until then, I continued to drop her till the auto stand every day, to spend as much time with her as possible.

Radhika's birthday was around the corner and I was confused about what to gift her.

'Let's get her a greeting card,' Kavya advised.

'What kind of card?'

'Pick a proposal card. It would have some nice love poem written on it. You just have to pen down your name.'

'Hmm, what about the birthday gift, Kavya?'

She left the bed and started pacing the room. I pulled out the emergency stock of cigarettes and handed it to her. She passed a winning smile. I closed the door, opened the window and sat on her bed while she puffed the tobacco stick.

'Do one thing! Book a dinner table in a five-star restaurant. At the end of the birthday celebration, give your proposal card to her.'

'That's it? I think we should buy something unique for her. And economical as well.'

'Yes,' Kavya agreed, getting back to her thinking mode and smoking a cigarette.

She passed a naughty grin and finished the cigarette. Confidence was smeared all over her face, which meant that she had cracked the puzzle.

'Lover boy, you need to gift her a cute little puppy which can remind her about you.'

'What kind of gift is that?'

'A cute little puppy will always be dear to her.'

'Is that the best you can suggest? A pet will just be an unnecessary responsibility.'

'So? Every relationship has some responsibility!'

A smile crept up on my face. We both understood the plan.

•

We went to the gift shop and explored a few options. Finally, we selected a card which read:

I love the way you make me smile.

Love you, my girl.

Now, we needed to buy a cute puppy.

Kavya and I went to a pet shop. We walked towards the last cabin and a few dogs barked at us. Every dog was caged, with a fancy aluminium bowl that had been kept for feeding.

'We need a small puppy,' Kavya said.

'How old?' the owner asked.

Kavya looked at me and then said, 'A few months old!'

The owner walked to the basement and we followed him. The room had more than a dozen puppies. I stroked the head of a cute one that was wagging his tail excitedly.

'You are so cute.' I touched its hairy tail and then started playing with it.

'We are not here for fun,' Kavya almost shouted, reminding me that I was there to choose one for Radhika, not myself.

The dog owner started pointing at different puppies, updating us alongside, 'This is German, American, Golden Retriever and Pomeranian.'

'Could you also tell the cost?'

'All are above fifty thousand, except two.'

I looked at Kavya and she blinked her eyes. I shrugged in helplessness.

Kavya slowly twisted her neck and asked the shop owner, 'Which are those two?'

He went to the corner and pointed at a black puppy and a white one.

'Which breed?' Kavya asked.

'The Indian breed is the cheapest. The white one is for three thousand and the other one is for two thousand.'

'Why is the black puppy cheaper?' I asked.

'White puppies are more in demand, that's why. We price according to demand and supply, madam,' he told my sister.

I picked the white one and stroked my hands over him. He wagged his tail and I whispered, looking at Kavya, 'I guess Radhika will like the white one.'

Kavya was unmoved. It seemed she was struggling hard to voice something.

'What happened? You did not like the puppy?'

Kavya picked the black one and said, 'This one also looks cute.'

'No!'

'Give her this black puppy, Vasu. Radhika will *have* to like the black one.'

'But why?'

She shrugged this time and pursed her lips.

'Why does she have to like the black puppy?'

'Because you are a dark man,' said the dog seller.

13

Hunk

The night before her birthday, I called Radhika around 11:45 p.m. I wanted to be the first one to wish her, but her phone was busy. My heart pounded against my chest, thinking about whom she was talking to at this hour.

I clenched my fists and gritted my teeth. I was restlessly pacing back and forth, my shoulders drooping in despair. I kept on looking at my phone with the hope that Radhika might call back.

I took a long breath and closed my eyes. My mind was filled with disturbing thoughts. My favourite person was getting closer to someone else. Out of anxiety, I covered my face with my palm. I called up Radhika again. Her phone was still busy.

I looked at Kavya. She was half asleep. After a few minutes, I received her message: *Thanks for the birthday wishes, but I cannot pick your call right now.*

I read her message thrice for the words to sink in. Then, I switched off the light and silently dozed off.

•

The next morning, I called Radhika and wished her.

'Hi Radhika! Happy birthday.'

'Hey! Many thanks, Vasu.'

'How is the day looking? Anything special planned up?'

'Nothing special. Papa did not even wish me.'

'Oh really! That's sad.'

'Frankly speaking, I was missing you last night.'

'Seriously? Why?' Suddenly, a rush of happiness hit my heart.

'I was thinking about how you had celebrated my last birthday in the class.'

'Radhika, I have planned something special for you today. Will you be free in the evening?'

'Sorry Vasu. Some of my friends are asking for a dinner party to celebrate my birthday.'

'Don't worry. You can call them as well.'

'Are you sure?'

'Yes, Radhika!'

'Where shall I call them?'

Window Grills, the pool restaurant in the Trident hotel opposite Jal Mahal.'

'Really?'

'Yes.'

'But that is an expensive place, Vasu.'

'Come on, I can do at least that much for you.'

●

'How would I propose to her in the presence of all her friends?' I said and looked at Kavya for some help. She was busy playing with the puppy. She had tied a soft red ribbon around its neck. The sticker read, "Hunk".

'Hunk? What kind of name is that?'

'You are a handsome hunk, lover boy.' She winked.

On Kavya's advice, I had applied a sandalwood face pack mixed with rose water. I washed my face after half an hour and it looked rejuvenated. Then, she gave me a face cream.

After massaging my face with the cream, I asked, 'How am I looking?'

'You always look great, Vasu.'

I wore a white and green striped shirt and gazed at my reflection in the mirror. Not satisfied with my look, I decided to change the shirt. Finally satisfied with a pale blue shirt, I picked up Hunk and placed him in a basket. I carried him to the back seat of my car. I parked the car two houses away from her place and called her.

Radhika was dressed in a knee-length white gown, flaunting her high heels. It was her plump lips tainted with red lipstick that caught my attention. She was shining like the moon against the dark night.

I was lost for words; she looked like an angel. I passed an awkward hug and wished her.

'Oh! You came by car today?' she asked excitedly. 'You could have told me before, Vasu. I might have dressed differently.'

'You are looking great, Radhika.'

It was hard for me to take my eyes off her. Her entire body seemed to be radiating an ethereal glow.

I drove the car and played some light romantic music. My dream girl was sitting beside me and I was taking her to a five-star hotel. I could not wait to confess my feelings to her.

•

As we reached the hotel, I noticed that the staff at the gate greeted Radhika, but no one acknowledged me. When we entered the main lobby, an attendant immediately came to open the door for Radhika while another one came to my side and said, 'Taxi parking is that side, sir.'

'But I am not a taxi driver. It is a private car.'

'But it's a taxi!' He pointed at my yellow taxi plate number.

Radhika and I exchanged a look of embarrassment. I silently drove to the taxi area and parked the car. I picked the basket and walked towards the entrance. As I stepped inside, the manager requested, 'Could you please put the basket under the X-ray scanner?'

I opened the basket for him. He looked at my surprise gift and shouted, 'Pets are not allowed.'

'Sir, today is her birthday. It is a gift for her.'

This was the second spoiler of the day. Radhika opened the basket and the adorable Hunk wagged its tail. Upon seeing Hunk, Radhika grabbed it and exclaimed with delight. 'It is so cute!'

The manager neared me and whispered, 'Is she your girlfriend?'

I nodded.

'Really!' He gave a judgemental look to me.

I nodded again.

'I will allow, but you must sit in the corner. If the puppy makes noise, you will have to remove him from the scene.'

I was happy that they gave us the corner seat. The restaurant overlooked the Aravalli Hills and offered exclusive Indian cuisine with live grills and traditional Kalbelia dance in a picturesque setting. It was a wonderful milieu for a romantic dinner.

When we entered the restaurant, Radhika opened the basket and said, 'I want to meet my birthday gift!'

Her smile made me forget all the troubles the day had given me. I decided to give the proposal card now, before the arrival of unwanted guests. I was almost ready to pull out the card when her phone rang.

'Hello, where are you?'

My ears were burning.

'You can come to the ground floor. We are already here,' Radhika said to the caller.

I decided to postpone the great proposal and wait for her friends. Then, Radhika shouted, 'Sanju!'

He waved his hand and walked towards us. He was holding a big plastic bag. Radhika hugged him and I closed my eyes. He was one of those few people who looked smarter in real life than his Facebook profile picture.

We exchanged an awkward hug and introduced ourselves. He sat in the middle chair. It seemed as if Sanju was a wall between me and Radhika.

'Are more people coming?' I asked.

'No, I have my best people here with me,' Radhika said with a pleasant smile

'Let's cut the cake first,' Sanju said and gave the box to the waiter. His dapper looks, smart clothes and expensive shoes seemed to have pitched him as my competitor for becoming Radhika's boyfriend.

The waiter came with a decorated cake with Radhika's name written on it. She cut the cake and offered the first bite to Sanju.

'Let's order wine,' Sanju suggested.

'But Radhika doesn't drink,' I said with knit brows.

'I already had one a few days ago, but in limited quantity.'

'Really?' I asked, surprised.

'Come on, Vasu! It's my birthday.'

Sanju signalled the waiter and said, 'Red wine.'

'Which brand, sir?'

'What are the options?'

'Shiraz Cabernet by Sula, Fratelli Sette, Big Banyan Merlot, Four Seasons Barrique Reserve Shiraz.'

My lips parted with surprise on hearing such difficult names.

When the wine was served, we raised a toast and cheered for Radhika. She initiated some trivial discussion about the computer professor and Sanju listened with rapt attention. He was continuously looking at her as they were busy talking to each other.

Finally, we ordered dinner. I did not even notice what I ate as I was disheartened to see how the evening had unfolded for me. At last, Sanju gifted Radhika a decorated box which had Swarovski label on it. It was a branded bracelet which had a rhodium-plated design. It was shimmering with sparkling pavé and delicate marquise-shaped stones.

A noise diverted my attention towards Hunk. I opened the basket as Hunk was feeling suffocated.

'I cannot take such an expensive gift, Sanju.'

Sanju held her palm and said, 'It is not that expensive, Radhika. I bought it for you.'

My jaw dropped. I was struggling to breathe. I glanced at my black Hunk. He was looking at me and wagging his tail.

No one likes the black puppy even if you are a Hunk.

14

Face Value

I decided to not share the birthday dinner details with Kavya. She was already occupied with her professional life and had very little time to guide me in my love story. Though Kavya had never shared her dilemma, I knew that she was struggling to find her life partner through the matrimonial site.

I continued to drop Radhika to the auto stand daily. However, that day Radhika was silent. She walked out of her house without a smile. Her eyes were lowered. She silently sat at the back seat of my scooty.

After a few minutes, she muffled, 'Hey, Vasu! I am thankful to you.'

'Thankful? For what?' I asked, carefully driving on the busy road.

'Nothing!'

Seeing her dejected look, I asked, 'Are you alright?'

'Dad is not keeping well. He is getting worse with every passing day.'

'Is it related to his drinking problem?'

She nodded. Her response was enough for me to understand that she was carrying the weight of innumerable hurdles.

We reached the last stop, but she requested, 'Could you drop me till the next crossing?'

'But you will not get an auto from there.'

'I am not going by auto today.'

I dropped her at the requested destination. She stepped down slowly and said, 'I will go on my own.'

'Are you going to a movie?'

'No, actually Sanju is coming here to receive me.'

'But I can drop you. Why have you called him?'

'Our path is very different. You are taking too much trouble for me.'

Her words hit me hard, but I could only feign a smile in response. We gazed at each other for a few seconds. Her face was brimming with empathy.

'So Sanju and you have the same path?' I asked.

A man on a bullet halted near us. He was wearing a trendy helmet and the bike was producing a deafening sound. I did not like the bike or his helmet. I did not like the man at all.

I swallowed hard and passed a cold stare. Sanju smiled back at me and I gave him a brief nod.

'Have a great day, Vasu.' Radhika quickly walked towards Sanju and did not wait for my reply.

I stood there for a few minutes. She sat pillion on his bike, gripped his right shoulder and turned to face me.

I passed an awkward smile. Then, the bullet moved ahead with a jerk and slowly, Radhika vanished in the crowd.

•

In the meantime, I had finished my graduation and joined Jai Mahal hotel as an associate. Kavya got her first promotion in her job. Now, her profile was uploaded on three different websites – Jeevansaathi.com, Shaadi.com, and Bharatmatrimony.com. Dad advised upgrading the Shaadi.com membership plan from gold to diamond. I read the benefits of the diamond membership that promised verified contact details, special offers from partners, sending direct messages to members and connecting instantly via Shaadi Chat Quick Response Services.

I sighed in disappointment and bit my lips. It felt like we were selling something that no one was ready to buy. It was hard to face the harsh reality.

Dad updated my number on these matrimonial portals as he did not want to share Kavya's number on a public forum. We had received several notifications where the families showed interest, but things never moved beyond a few conversations. Most of them asked for Kavya's pictures, but they never called us back.

One such Sunday, Dad invited a family for lunch. Kavya had already interacted with the boy on text messages and the family had spoken to dad twice. We were hopeful for this alliance.

Dad said that they were coming just for a casual lunch, but everyone knew that nothing was "casual" about this lunch.

The sofa covers were washed. The curtains were replaced with brand new ones and all the unwanted things were shifted to the storeroom. Suddenly, there was so much space around the room. Mom opened a brand new set of kitchen crockery. I had seldom seen such elaborate preparations, even for Diwali.

A list of items was handed over to me which mostly included sweets and assorted salted snacks. Mr Singh, along with his wife and his son, came in the afternoon. Dad welcomed them in the drawing-room and mom advised Kavya to stay in her room until she was called downstairs. A series of trivial conversations happened, along with the introductions of the family members.

'How is your business going?' the boy's father asked dad.

'Not very great! I have nine cars now, but it's mostly a seasonal business.'

We only had seven taxis, but I was surprised how my father added two new cars on the spot. They spent half an hour discussing about the business, job opportunities and latest smartphone models. They even expressed concerns about the emerging women fashion trends which were threatening our traditions. I wondered whether they were here to see Kavya or for striking a business deal.

'Where is Kavya?' Finally, the boy's mom enquired.

'Vasu, go bring Kavya. Hope she is ready.'

'Kavyaaa...' I screamed.

'Vasu, go to her room and escort her here,' mom whispered angrily.

Both the women looked at each other and smiled. I went to call Kavya. She was dressed in a new green suit. Her face had a thick layer of makeup that made her look artificial. Her eyes were lined with kohl and she was wearing a new jewellery set, which was very rare in her case.

I escorted Kavya and wondered why I needed to do it in my own house. She walked painfully slowly, offered namaste and sat with mom.

There was an awkward silence for a few seconds. Then, the family started scanning Kavya.

'If you want to ask anything from Kavya, you can ask,' my father said. It looked like she was here for the interview.

'Have you ever been to your hometown?' Mrs Singh asked.

'No, I have only been to Jaipur and Udaipur,' Kavya said, gazing at the ground and using precise words to answer their questions.

I wondered if I would have asked the same question, she might have written a book to explain.

All the three guests gazed at Kavya as if she was a Monalisa painting, hung at some museum.

'The boy and girl should get to know each other,' his mom said.

'Of course!' Dad agreed.

Suddenly, the boy received a call. He left the sofa and went to a corner. He was looking more at us than talking on the phone.

He finished the call and said, 'I will have to leave as there is an emergency.'

Mr Singh nodded. The boy almost ran away, as if he had been forced to come here. There was a brief silence in the room. We looked at each other. Everyone was struggling hard to interpret what had happened.

Kavya rose and silently moved to her room. Meanwhile, dad urged the guests to join for lunch. While having lunch, they said, 'Nowadays, Facebook is so misleading. People look so different on social media,' Mrs Singh said.

Once the meal was wrapped up, dad called me over. 'Vasu, can you please drop Mrs and Mr Singh in our car?'

Mom mumbled to dad, 'Why are you sending Vasu to drop them? Can't they go by taxi?' But dad did not answer.

After formal namastes and goodbyes, I was finally alone in the car with them.

•

'How long have you guys been searching for a groom for Kavya?' Mr Singh asked.

'Two years.'

'Good! Your father is an intelligent man to have started the hunt early. At least this will give them more time to find the perfect match.'

'But why search more? You liked Kavya, right?'

'It's not about me, Vasu. It's about my son.'

Mr Singh turned back, exchanged a glance with his wife, and politely said, 'Seems like you have not understood the matter.'

I shrugged.

'My son rejected Kavya.'

'Really?'

It brought a smile on my face as I did not want her to get married and leave so soon.

'Tell Kavya to put her original pictures on Facebook. It's so misleading,' Mrs Singh said.

'Misleading? How?'

'She looks decent on Facebook. But, in reality, she is so different.'

'So, being different is wrong?'

'No, we are not saying that. But everyone wants to marry someone who belongs to the same caste, class and social status. Most importantly, the person should have a pleasant appearance.'

I tried to decipher her words as I was a little late to understand everything. The Google map informed that we would be reaching our destination in three minutes. I decided to reason with them.

'So, a handsome boy should marry a good-looking girl only?'

'Yes, at least in an arranged marriage.'

'What about love marriage?'

He flared his nostrils and said, 'Love is blind!'

The same evening, I was sitting on my bed, checking my Facebook profile on my new smartphone. Then, I clicked on Radhika's profile and wondered how was her profile misleading. I went to my friend list and typed Kavya, but nothing appeared.

'Hey Kavya! I cannot see your Facebook account. Did you block me?'

'No, I have deleted my Facebook account.' I was shocked.

'Why did you do that?'

'I don't want people to judge me on the basis of my photos,' she said. Then, she picked a few books from the bed and threw them on the table. Her agitation was palpable. Finally, she switched off the light and covered herself under the quilt.

I shut down the laptop and went to comfort her.

'Facebook is all about face value, Kavya.'

She uncovered her face and shouted, 'I want people to value me, not my face.'

The discussion ended there, but Kavya never activated her profile on Facebook ever again.

15

The Hug

The rejection had done more damage to Kavya than I had anticipated. She did not speak to anyone for days. She stopped looking at the matrimonial sites. Dad gave the login details of the matrimonial sites to me as he was unable to handle the activity. I often logged in to see the matches, but did not discuss them with Kavya as I did not want to hurt her.

One day, I was watching my all-time favourite movie *Kung Fu Panda* when my phone vibrated. It was a WhatsApp message from Radhika.

If you are free, let us meet at the Krishna temple at 6 p.m. It has been long since we visited the temple together.

I immediately picked up a basic plain shirt and wore the stone-washed jeans. I wondered if it would give an impression of a reckless personality. Then, I decided that it was best to stick to single colour jeans and pair them with a crisp plain shirt. To complete my smart look, I wore the formal derby shoes. Once I was ready, I gazed at myself in the mirror. I noticed that as always, my teeth shone brighter than my face.

A smile appeared on my face. My mind knew that this time around, there would not be any Sanju.

Radhika came to the temple with a smiling face and we both offered our prayers. I closed my eyes and had an internal conversation with Krishna. 'Please forgive me for not showing much interest in you today.'

When I opened my eyes, Radhika was still praying. I gazed at Krishna and Radha. I recollected that Krishna had so many gopis. I felt a tinge of sympathy for Radha.

We stepped out of the temple and Radhika suggested we have some tea. We strolled a few steps and Radhika pointed at a tea shop, 'Let's have tea there?'

I nodded. I did not want to go there with Radhika, as the tea stall was surrounded by rowdy boys. I ordered tea and five pairs of eyes were staring at Radhika. She turned around and shrugged. I guess she did not care much as she looked worried.

'What happened, Radhika? You look upset today.'

'My graduation is over and dad will not send me for higher studies. Instead, he wants me to get married.'

'But we are just twenty-two.'

'He says I am old enough.'

'What are your other friends doing?'

'Sanju is going for his Master's degree.'

I flared my nostrils at Sanju's mention.

'You can also pursue MCA, Radhika.'

'But we don't have money. All the money is reserved for my dad's treatment and my wedding.'

'Is there any way in which I can help you?'

'Can you ask Kavya to assist me in finding a job in the field of computer science? That would be a great help, Vasu!'

'Sure, I will try my best.'

'Thanks.' She put her hand on my shoulder.

'So, you are not going to study more?'

She shook her head.

'You should study more.'

'We belong to a middle-class family, Vasu. Sadly, a middle-class family is more worried about their daughter's wedding than her education.'

•

It was an early Sunday morning. Everyone was still asleep, while I was lying awake on my bed. A notification appeared on my phone. It was from Radhika.

My eyes widened upon reading her name. She had called me as well, but I was unable to pick her call. I read the message.

Hey, good morning. Please reply if you are awake.

I called Radhika immediately.

'Hey, Radhika. You called me?'

'Yes, sorry to disturb you so early in the morning. Can you please come with me to the airport?'

'Sure.'

It was 5:00 a.m. I was so delighted to talk to her that I did not even ask her the reason for visiting the airport so early in the morning.

Kavya woke up and demanded an answer. 'Sorry, Kavya. I got a call from Radhika.'

She showed her middle finger to display her anger and went back to sleep.

I brushed my teeth, got ready, picked up the car keys and walked out. Radhika was already standing outside the house.

'What happened, Radhika? All well?'

'Yes! Let's rush to the airport first, please. Departure, Jaipur International Airport.'

•

The sky was clear, but it was still dark. The roads were empty and only a few cyclists and fitness enthusiasts could be seen.

'Why are we going to the airport?' I finally asked.

'Actually, Sanju is going to the USA and I want to see him off.'

My legs froze. It seemed as if the car had refused to move forward and the speed was mechanically reduced. I parked my car at the roadside.

'What happened? Why did you stop the car, Vasu?'

'I need to use the washroom, sorry.'

'Please be fast,' she said while texting on her phone.

I went to the Sulabh complex and took the maximum time there. I never thought I had so much water or frustration stored within me. I finished everything in ten minutes, came out and started the car. My next stop was the petrol pump.

'What happened now, Vasu?' she said in an agitated voice.

'I need diesel. The tank is almost empty!'

'Oh, Vasu! I guess I would miss him.' She looked very sad and I could not bear to see her like that. I paid for the fuel and drove to the airport.

When we reached, she got down from the car and I went to the parking area. I did not want Sanju and Radhika to meet each other. I was waiting and killing time by seeing all the other taxi drivers. I bumped my leg on the front wheel and hit the car.

My breath was heavy as I was getting restless. Patience is not simply the ability to wait, it is how we behave while we are waiting. That day, I realized that I lacked patience.

I got a call and instantly pressed the green button.

'Hey Vasu, where are you? Please come over to Gate A. Sanju's flight got delayed.'

'I am in the parking area.'

'No! Please come. Sanju wants to meet you. He is going abroad for two years.'

Two years! These words gave a new lease of life to my dead soul.

I walked to the entry gate and met Sanju. We exchanged a hug and I asked, 'Hey, Sanju! Why are you going suddenly?'

'I took admission at California State University to pursue MBA, man.'

'Oh! That is great news. We will miss you, though!' I said with a wicked grin.

Looking at his phone, Sanju said, 'I should go now to avoid the last minute rush.'

'Sure,' Radhika said.

He hugged her again and said, 'Thanks for bringing her here. And please take care of my Radhika.'

My Radhika! The words pierced through my heart.

Radhika was silent. She was gazing at the ground. Then, Sanju slowly lifted her chin and said, 'Radhika, look at me!'

Tears had pooled up in her eyes. Her cheeks flushed, making her appear like a pink doll. Sanju cupped her face and they stared at each other. My heart started beating rapidly. I formed a fist and controlled my emotions. I thought he was going to kiss Radhika, but thankfully, they just hugged each other.

Sanju was calm, but Radhika was in tears. I was not required there anymore. I closed my eyes and walked towards the parking.

•

After taking Radhika to the airport, I came home and went straight to my room. I lay on my bed and covered myself completely under the bed sheet. Then, I closed my eyes and silently vanished into the realm of my turbulent thoughts. The entire episode of the airport replayed in my mind. I was disheartened to see how Sanju had hugged Radhika. Her teary-eyed face kept resurfacing again and again.

'Where did you go so early in the morning?'

I removed the bed sheet and found Kavya standing over me.

'That is none of your business.'

I pulled the sheet back over my face. She gently removed the bed sheet again and asked, 'Are you okay, Vasu?'

'No, I am not!'

'What happened?'

I uncovered my face and screamed, 'She hugged him.'

'Radhika hugged Sanju? But why?'

I refused to speak further as I was trying hard to control my emotions. Kavya switched off the cooler and turned on the fan. I felt suffocated. I removed the bedsheet for fresh air.

Kavya was still staring at me. 'Can we talk?'

She again stroked my head, but I didn't utter a word. She went out and returned with a glass of lemonade. I drank it and started feeling better.

'Don't say anything related to Radhika,' I requested.

'Okay, I will not.'

Kavya tried to read my puppy face. She gazed at me with sympathy and said, 'Do you need a hug?'

'Fuck off! Go hug your Sanju.'

Kavya left the bed and started walking around the room.

'I don't need any more tricks, Kavya. I have lost the battle.'

'What does it mean, Vasu?' I could not hold back and told her everything. My eyes were brimming with streams of tears.

She heard me patiently and took me in a warm hug. 'Don't ever say that you have lost the battle, Vasu.'

'But that is the fact, Kavya.'

'You are never so lost that you could not fight again.'

I frowned. She was not making sense at all. Kavya started walking around in the room. She gazed at me twice and then, passed an almost evil grin.

'What happened? Why are you smiling like that?'

'When you think all is lost, that's when life gives you a hint. You need to be smart enough to understand and take action.'

'What is the hint here? That they hugged each other, like a couple? I saw Radhika's love for Sanju in her eyes.'

'It was a departing hug, bro!'

'You have no idea how desperate she was to meet him.'

'But suppose, she will be sad tomorrow, whose shoulder would she cry on?'

I narrowed my vision and tried to read her. She neared me and put a hand on my shoulder.

'Suppose she needs a hug, who will be there to hug her?'

'Maybe me, Kavya. But I am a friend.'

'Sanju is gone for two years and a long-distance relationship doesn't work. What if he finds a better American girl there?'

'So, what does that mean?'

'It means that you have *two years* to become her boyfriend. Sanju is gone so there would be no one to obstruct you from reaching your goal.'

'But, is it right?'

'Please understand that you are not replacing anyone. You are just making your presence felt a little more in her life.'

'Then what should I do?'

'You have to behave like a shoulder and keep on supporting her in crisis. One day she will be yours.'

'What if she denies my love, Kavya?'

'Remember Vasu, winners win the trophy, but losers win hearts.'

'But I want to win the trophy too.'

She rolled her eyes and said, 'Oh, my poor lover boy!'

16

A Heart of Gold

Kavya Speaks

I have seen Vasu going through many adversities. He is a strong and resilient boy, who has faced every hurdle with courage. However, the day he returned from the airport, I found him at his lowest point in life. He told me everything that had happened at the airport – how Radhika had hugged Sanju lovingly, how her eyes were filled with affection for him and most importantly, how they were a couple. It was obvious that a girl like Radhika would never settle for a boy like Vasu.

I motivate Vasu and challenge him to never give up in life. I know he deserves all the happiness in the world, which is why I want to protect him from heartbreaks and grief. But this time, I played a very dangerous game. I knew from the beginning that Vasu had nothing better to offer compared to Sanju. And yet, I pushed him to date Radhika.

When a bird learns to fly, it doesn't do so because it has a destination in mind. It flies to discover the strength of its wings. The bird holds on to the faith that the winds will carry it to where it belongs.

Just like that, in life, we may not know where we are headed, but our strong wings and the winds of time will take us to our destination.

Vasu may not have anything better to offer than Sanju, but he has a heart of gold, which is priceless in today's world.

17

The Emergency

Narendra Modi was unanimously elected as the new Indian Prime Minister. The skilful way in which he managed to sweep clean the seats in the elections was one of the most talked-about news events in 2014. Dad had got a new business website designed with the name – Meena International Travels. It was a major move as it had opened doors for foreign tourists to avail our services online.

Since our family business was flourishing, Kavya and I became more involved in supporting dad. I was handling logistics while Kavya managed digital services. She also helped Radhika get a job at the Aptech Coaching Centre as a teacher.

Meanwhile, I had started working at The Jai Mahal Resort as an associate. I was responsible for event management, business generation, promotions and other social events. The job turned out to be a perfect opportunity for me to hone my soft skills. While managing events, I got a chance to work with different kinds of people which enhanced my interpersonal talents. My boss was impressed with the way I performed my responsibilities as I received a lot of appreciation from my clients. In this role, I discovered a new Vasu – a confident and smart boy who had the ability to cultivate enduring relationships.

I often tried to drop Radhika at the coaching centre. Sanju's absence had definitely brought us closer. Our bond was becoming stronger than ever.

It was Navratri and we were all geared up for the puja ceremonies. On the eighth day, mom had invited all the relatives and guests to celebrate the auspicious occasion. But this time, she sent a special invitation to Radhika's family as Kavya had managed to persuade her to call them. Our parents had already met each other in school gatherings before. But Radhika was coming to my home for the first time and I was on cloud nine. This Navratri turned out to be truly festive for me!

When they came in the evening, I was at my best behaviour. I asked Radhika's mom about her health and even appreciated her saree. She was delighted to talk to me. She even thanked me for arranging a part-time job for Radhika. The smile on my face knew no bounds.

Did Radhika's family like me?

Radhika sat with me during the entire puja. She even took a selfie with me from her bulky smartphone and posted it on Instagram. When I saw the image, I realized that her fair complexion was matched only by my radiant teeth. But when she posted the picture on Instagram, she applied so many filters that a new version of me was visible with her. I was looking fairer. Her picture caption read – *Celebrating Navratri with my best friend.*

'When did you buy a new phone?' I asked, looking at her phone.

'Oh! This one was gifted to me by Sanju. He ordered it online.'

My face froze in an instant. When I checked Instagram, Radhika's pictures had already received 400 likes and ten comments – *Radhika, you are looking beautiful, looking fresh, nice click...*

I had never seen my image getting so many comments or likes. I sighed and closed Instagram.

One night I dreamt that Radhika was in a wedding dress. She was walking leisurely with a smiling face towards me. The relatives were showering flowers on her. I was pleased that I was with Radhika and there was no Sanju to interrupt us.

I was immersed in this beautiful dream when my phone rang, and it diverted my attention. I silenced the phone as I did not want anything to come in between my one-sided fantasies but it rang again. I checked the time and it was showing 11:30 p.m. I checked the caller. A smile ran on my face, but before I could pick it, the call got disconnected. She called me again after another minute. It was Radhika's call.

'Hi, Radhika! How are you?'

'Vasu, I need your help.'

'What happened?'

'Please come fast. It is my dad!' She hung up, without even completing the sentence.

I jumped out of the blanket and rushed out. Upon reaching Radhika's house, I learned that Radhika's father had suffered a heart attack and she had tried calling three hospitals for an ambulance, with no luck. I lifted him with her help, settled him in the car and rushed him to the nearest hospital. As soon as we reached the hospital, the emergency staff started the treatment.

Eventually, the doctors managed to revive him. They shifted him to the ICU for observation. Radhika's mother was inconsolable and Radhika was ferrying between her parents.

Since I had been woken up by Radhika early that morning, I did not realize when I fell asleep in the lobby.

'Vasu, can you drop mom home?'

I rubbed my eyes and asked, 'What about you?'

'I will stay here.'

'You must be tired.'

'No, I can manage.'

Before getting down from the car, Radhika's mother requested, 'Can you please come after an hour? I need to give you something?' I nodded and went home.

When I entered home, Kavya was already waiting for me. She examined me from top to bottom and asked, 'What happened? Why didn't you go to the office today?'

I told her about Radhika's dad and the emergency. After listening to everything, Kavya placed a hand on my shoulder and smiled.

'Now what's cooking behind that smile?'

'Lover boy, no one can come and help so soon, especially from America.'

I smiled back.

•

After an hour, I went to Radhika's house. Her mother had packed a few sandwiches and tea in a thermal bottle. I took them and drove towards the hospital. Radhika was busy typing something on the phone. I peeked at her phone screen and one line caught my attention – *Thanks to Vasu.*

For the first time, I was not jealous of Sanju.

'How is uncle doing?'

Radhika closed the chat and said, 'He is fine.'

'Aunty has given some sandwiches and tea. Please eat something. You must be hungry!'

She nodded and we went to the hospital cafeteria. As she took the first bite of her sandwich, I decided to distract her from the present crisis.

'How is Hunk, Radhika?'

'Hunk is very cute. He is really dear to me.'

'Your father doesn't have any brothers or friends? No one is here to see him.'

'Papa is an alcoholic. Once he is high, he cannot control himself. He has fought with almost everyone.'

'Oh.'

'Actually I am not close to dad. His condition does not make much difference to me.'

I fidgeted and settled back. Back in school, I had never imagined that she was going through so much in her life.

Radhika finished her sandwich and said, 'Thank you, Vasu.' Actually, I am more worried about mom. What will happen to her if I marry and leave?'

'You don't have to worry about that. I will always be there.'

We finished the sandwiches and I got up to leave. But then, I noticed that Radhika was still sitting on the chair and was looking at me. It bothered me as I couldn't understand what was running in her mind. Then, she came closer and hugged me.

'You are just like Hunk. He always hugs me and never makes me feel alone.'

I was too lost in our hug to understand what she was saying. After all, she had hugged me for the first time.

'I'll be there for you,' I whispered.

'Even if the world changes, you don't change, Vasu.'

18

The Boy with a Tattoo

As the years passed by, the travel industry changed drastically, because of corporate giants like Make My Trip, Yatra.com, Clear Trip and several others. These travel companies had plenty of airlines and travel partners to help travellers plan perfectly within their budgets. As a result, dad's business was badly hit.

Around this time, we got a booking for a group of Israeli tourists who wanted to visit Rajasthan. To help my dad, I went to the Jaipur airport to receive them.

Once I reached there, I stood at the exit gate, holding the placard with "Meena International Travel" printed on it. Whenever I saw a foreigner, I gave a congenial smile and said, 'Welcome to India!'

While assisting the Israeli tourists, I observed that they all had giant and eccentric tattoos on their bodies. Each of them was patterned with different designs, colours and even texts. My gaze fell on a fair girl's belly. She had a tattoo to the left and the tattooed text said, "Flip it and taste it." Even though I was getting more curious about this strange phenomenon, I refrained from looking at it more.

I interacted with them to know more about their culture and lifestyle. In one of the conversations, they told me that they were visiting India for the first time and were looking forward to it.

•

Kavya had been busy at the bank for the whole week. So, by Saturday night, she was exhausted to the bones. She wanted to unwind, so we locked the room from inside and opened the bottle of vodka and breezer that I had secretly purchased in the afternoon. Vodka was too strong for me, but Kavya had demanded it. I guess she could drink anything. Whenever I would fail to finish the drink, she did it for me. It was our weekly celebration ritual.

Once we had settled ourselves with our drinks, Kavya asked, 'So, when are you going to propose to her? '

'Has the time come for it?'

'This is the best time. Her mom also likes you.'

'Should I tell mom to talk to them about the wedding?'

'Are you crazy? First, you have to win the girl.'

I exhaled and she understood that I was very scared.

'Don't worry, I will help you.'

'Thank you, didi.'

'Don't patronize me by calling me didi.'

'You are right, Kavya. Suggest some good ways to propose.'

'Hmm! How about a letter or poem?'

'From where will I get a nice poem?'

'I can find some good poems for you from Google.'

She finished the bottle of vodka and passed a nasty burp. 'You need to do something unique, Vasu.'

I tried to recollect all the romantic movies and counted my options. There was love letters, greeting cards, poetry or a public announcement on the speaker. Suddenly, the tattooed Israeli guests came into my mind.

'Can I propose with a tattoo?'

'Tattoo? What kind of tattoo?'

'One that would say, "Radhika, I love you"?'

'Wow, that is a good idea!'

'Now where should I have the tattoo?'

Before Kavya could answer, she passed out on my bed. I think vodka finally won over her.

'Hey, Kavya! Where should I have the tattoo?'

She did not move. I nudged her and asked again.

She fidgeted and opened her right eye. She said, 'You have a golden heart, Vasu.' And then, she collapsed again.

•

Jaipur was witnessing a burgeoning tattoo culture. A whole lot of tattoo artists had come up in a short span of time, so it wasn't difficult for me to find a studio.

When I walked in, I saw the photos of their customers which were displayed on the wall. There were various tattoos – a few bird designs, some colourful animals, calligraphic texts, and a colourful heart. My eyes landed on a white girl who had a tattoo on her breast. My jaw dropped with awe.

'I inked that design,' the artist said, following my gaze. I was stunned.

'So where do you want the design?'

'I want to express my love to my girl.'

'Love comes from the heart, so you should have a tattoo on your chest,' he suggested.

'Good. What are the charges?'

'Tell me the design and length of the tattoo.'

'It should read, "I love you Radhika".'

'Want to propose to your girlfriend?' He grinned.

I nodded with a smile.

'Remove the t-shirt and lie down on this armchair.'

'What are the charges?'

'I need to check your skin type and the length of the tattoo. I guess the length should be five-inches. I charge one thousand rupees for one inch but I will give you some discount. You will have to pay just about three thousand.'

I nodded and removed my t-shirt. My dark naked body was shining in front of him. He tried to draw a few lines around my chest.

'Seems blue ink will not work for you.'

'Use white or red,' I suggested.

'I don't have white ink. Let's use dark red.'

He searched in his cupboard and pulled out the dark red pen. He drew a few lines on my chest and then advised, 'Let's keep the tattoo short. A long tattoo will not look good on your chest.'

'Okay. How to make it short?'

'Let's keep it "Love Radhika" if you agree? Then at the place of love, we can draw a small red-coloured heart.'

'Wow. That is a great idea.'

He applied some moisturizer over my chest. Then, he wore a pair of black gloves and pulled out the needle. I observed the needle and realized that embossing a tattoo was a bad idea.

'It will not hurt much.'

I took a long breath, gritted my teeth and held the rod of the reclining bed.

He inserted the needle and tattooed on my chest while I was on a painful journey. To endure the misery, I closed my eyes and recollected Radhika's smiling face.

While he was working, I opened my eyes. He looked at me and said with a grin, 'The heart is done.'

'Please give a black border if you can.'

He gestured towards the small, inked heart and said, 'Black border is already there.'

'Okay. Please go slow. Hope it will not pain much.'

Then, he pulled out another needle and started embossing RADHIKA. I was engrossed in my favourite dream where Radhika was the bride. I was sitting on the stage while she was walking towards me, holding a garland.

Suddenly the pain became intense and I wondered whether I was getting a heart attack. I opened my eyes and gave the tattoo artist a cold look. He was drenched in sweat.

Then, he took a long breath and said, 'Actually sir, the text is not looking good on your body.'

There was silence in the room. There was no point shouting at him, so I let out the breath I was holding and told him, 'Do one thing, at least write RADHA.'

'Good idea, you can start calling your girlfriend Radha and then propose to her.'

I gave him a cold stare.

Finally, after a long painful journey, I looked in the mirror and my blood-leaking chest with the name RADHA. It looked like I had murdered an entire army to get my Radha. The tattoo artist applied the bandage and instructed, 'Remove the bandage after one day. And gently wash the tattoo with antimicrobial soap. Keep on applying a moisturizer or ointment to keep it moist.'

The tattoo artist did not charge any money. So he gave me one reason to like the tattoo. I walked out with a smile.

•

I decided to surprise Kavya with my tattoo. In the evening, while she was on her bed surfing something on her phone, I said, 'I have an exciting surprise for you.'

'Surprise? I love surprises. Tell me fast.' She kept the phone on the bed.

I stood on the bed, looking like a thin and starved Hanuman. I unhooked two buttons of my shirt and shouted, 'Here you go!'

Kavya watched the tattoo and frowned. Then she touched it, slightly digging in her long nails.

'Ouch. It hurts, Kavya!'

'Is it a permanent tattoo?' she asked, still puzzled.

'Yes, do you like it?'

'Are you crazy?' Her volume pierced my ears.

She held her head in frustration. I wondered whether she was upset with the tattoo or with the message.

'Did you not like the tattoo?'

'No! This is horrible. And it is a permanent tattoo, Vasu! What if she does not accept your proposal?'

'But why would she do that?'

'Oh boy! When did you decide to do this?'

'Last night, when you were enjoying the drink. You encouraged me to go for it!'

'Vasu, never take any suggestion from someone who is drunk.'

19

A Great Loss

It was Saturday. I had decided to propose to Radhika outside the Radha Krishna temple. I had admired my tattoo thrice in the mirror since that morning. I was pleased to see that it was somewhat readable now. RADHA was a bit tough to read, but the red coloured heart was shining. I smiled, looking at my reflection.

Kavya was at the office and I was on a rotation off. The hotel industry had peak working hours on weekends so I had a free Saturday. While getting ready, I noticed that only half an hour was left to meet Radhika. Without delaying any further, I decided to leave for the temple, taking the bravest step of a lover's life. My emotions were not high but fear was.

When I reached the temple, I prayed for the success of my love. I had an internal dialogue with lord Krishna where I conveyed that just like he has Radha in his heart, my Radhika resides in my heart too. In fact, she has conquered it.

I sat on the stairs outside the temple, waiting for Radhika but she didn't arrive. I took out my phone and called her, but she did not answer. I even messaged her on WhatsApp, but she did not respond. After waiting for an hour, I decided to go to Radhika's house to check if everything was fine.

When I reached her building, I saw three bikes and a car parked outside. When I rang the bell, Radhika opened the door. Her hair was untidy and her eyes were red. I was surprised to see her dejected face. Before I could say anything, she came forward and hugged me.

'Vasu, I lost my father.'

It took a few seconds to register.

'What?' I asked, trying to comfort her.

We freed ourselves from the hug.

'He suffered a heart stroke in the afternoon. We called the ambulance, but by the time he reached the hospital, he was already gone. He could not survive, Vasu!'

•

The last rites of Radhika's father were conducted at the Durgapura cremation ground. I wanted to attend the ceremony but Kavya restricted me by saying that it would not be an easy sight for me. Women were not allowed in the cremation area so they all remained in the house. Mom went to see Radhika's mom. Kavya and I also went to express our condolences. The house was occupied with relatives, but still, there was a deadly silence. Even the naughty Hunk was sitting silently in one corner.

Radhika came and sat with us. I placed my hand on her shoulder, hoping to ease her pain. I could not bear to see her like this. Her face had lost its glow and her eyes were portraying the depth of her loss. I wished I could also do something for her. I was trying to say something but nothing came to my mind. The intense silence still prevailed.

'Uncle is in a good place, Radhika. May his soul rest in peace!' I said in a low voice.

Radhika flushed, 'No, he is not.'

I swallowed hard.

'Uncle must have gone to heaven. He was good at heart'

'Everybody wants to go to heaven, but nobody wants to die.'

'I know it is hard, but such is life. We cannot escape the pain of separation. But, it gets better with time.'

'I hate this life,' she replied sternly.

I controlled my voice and understood that I was bad at extending condolences. I concluded that she hated her father.

'Death ends all relationships, I guess,' I said.

'Death ends a life, not a relationship,' she replied.

20

Real Beauty

Radhika changed her WhatsApp display picture to that of her picture with her father. I had never seen her picture with him ever before. He was looking elated in the picture. I could feel how depressed Radhika might be feeling so I sent a few motivational quotes copied from Instagram, but she did not reply to me.

Surprisingly, Radhika had stopped responding to my calls and messages. I decided to give her some space to come to terms with her personal loss, even though I was having a tough time as I wanted to know how she was doing. I persisted and did not disturb her. After ten days, she finally texted me.

I am fine, Vasu.

Radhika has stopped going to her office as well. I was unable to extend a helping hand to comfort her. However, mom would often spend some time with her family. On asking about their state, she gave a feeble reply, as expected. I wanted to reach out to her, but she wanted to be left alone. I had no option but to wait patiently.

I had started working very hard in the hotel, which had a positive impact on my professional growth. Seeing my dedication, my boss started giving me important clients to manage.

On one such day when I was busy working at the hotel, I got a call from Radhika.

'Hi Radhika! How are you?'

Without responding to my pleasantries, she said, 'Vasu, are you free?'

'I'm at work. Anything urgent?'

'What time will you be free?'

'I can come to you in half an hour.'

'Meet me once you finish work. Come by car, if you can.'

She disconnected the call. I recollected the last time she had requested me to visit her by car. It was when she wanted to meet Sanju.

I took a deep breath and mumbled, 'Is Sanju back?'

•

When I reached Radhika's house, her mother opened the door.

'How are you, Vasu beta?'

'I am good, aunty. Is Radhika here?'

'Are you here for Radhika?' I nodded. 'But she does not want to meet anyone.'

'But *she* called me, aunty.'

A ray of hope emerged on her face.

'Radhika is mentally disturbed, Vasu. Please take care of her. I am glad she is willing to talk to you, but please do not discuss anything related to her father.'

I nodded and entered inside. A thin Radhika was standing in the drawing room with an artificial smile. She had lost weight and the glow of her face had vanished. Her hair was in disarray. Her dry lips and slouching posture spoke a lot. Her mother gave me a glass of water as I stood there, watching her.

Radhika said, 'Mom, I'm going to the temple.' She picked up her handbag and walked towards the door. When her mother came outside to close the main door, she gave a cold stare. I noticed her gaze, but didn't know what it meant. Finally, we sat in my car and I turned on the engine.

'Which temple do you want to go to, Radhika?'

'Anywhere. But it *does not* have to be a temple.'

I drove through Jaipur streets. It was late evening and roads were already flooded with people. Radhika unzipped her bag and pulled out two bottles. She poured whiskey into the half-filled cold drink plastic bottle. Then, she took a large sip and reclined on her seat comfortably.

'Vasu, can you please switch on the AC?'

The air conditioner was already on, so I lowered the temperature.

'Can we have something to eat? I am hungry.'

After a few turns, I parked the car outside a shop and brought two samosas and kachoris. Radhika took a large bite of the samosa. She was hogging as if she had been hungry for days.

'When did you start drinking like this, Radhika?'

She ignored my question and continued eating the samosa.

'Radhika, answer me!' I asserted.

'I've had many drinks like this before with Sanju.'

'Oh! But why are you drinking again?'

'Every child has to finish their father's unfinished business. I am finishing my father's leftover whiskey.'

'But it will harm you.'

'Who cares?'

'I care.'

'Only you care, Vasu,' she said angrily and held my gaze for a long time. 'But no one else cares.'

'Everyone cares for you.' I put my hand on her shoulder and tried to comfort her.

'I don't want anyone else. I want *him*. The person who left this country.'

'Sanju?'

'Don't take his name.'

I gulped and went silent. Her mom had asked me not to talk about her father, but it seemed she was missing someone else.

We remained quiet in my car for another half an hour. Radhika was savouring her snacks and drinks. I summoned my courage twice to speak, but she did not reply. We returned home late in the night.

•

Tough times always surprise us. Radhika lost her father, but her mother had developed a good friendship with my mom. One evening, Radhika's mother visited our home and mom instructed me to buy some snacks. I guessed they wanted to talk in isolation.

I brought home dhokla and a few other Indian snacks. I saw that both the women were engaged in a serious discussion in the kitchen.

'Why are you pushing her to marry?'

'She is upset and has started drinking as well. I need to get her settled soon.'

'But is she ready?'

'She *will be* ready. Her father wanted her to marry last year itself.'

'She is a good girl.'

I opened the snacks packet and started having it. Suddenly, the conversation got so interesting that I had finished half of the dhoklas in one go.

'What kind of boy are you looking for?' my mom asked.

I wanted to scream that I was available.

'I am looking for a good-looking and a well-settled boy. Somebody who would be a good match for my beautiful Radhika.'

'I wish Kavya was also a little fair.'

'But she is a smart girl. Don't worry! Kavya will also get a good husband,' Radhika's mother said.

My ears started burning. I kept the half-eaten snacks on the table and screamed, 'Mom, snacks are outside. Please have it.'

•

The same night, I was pondering how everyone wanted to marry a similar type of person. I tried hard to convince myself that looks don't matter. But maybe, they do.

'Kavya, why is a good-looking face so important for people in marriage?'

She dropped the phone and looked at me.

'Who said so?'

'That is not important.'

'Maybe because they have to see the same face for the rest of their life! So the prettier the face, the better it would be.'

'But external beauty does not last. We will grow old with time. Any pretty face will have wrinkles and the hair would fall.'

'Only a compassionate boy like you can understand this, Vasu. Intelligent fools don't.'

'What does that mean, Kavya?'

'People need a kind heart like yours to appreciate real beauty.'

21

An Unexpected News

Kavya had already faced the fourth rejection. Every time a boy's family came to see her, they brought with them a ray of hope. But in the end, they scurried off with a silent, cold reply. The struggle to get a perfect life partner was getting even more difficult for her. Now everyone was afraid of what would happen if the next boy also rejected Kavya. I often visited Radhika's home to support her family through their difficult phase. Radhika's mom had become very fond of me. She had started treating me like her own son.

It was a holiday and I was glued to the new TV in our room, watching the animated movie *Ice Age: Continental Drift*. I was giggling at the funny scenes when I got a call from Radhika's mother.

'Hey Vasu, are you free?'

'Yes, aunty.'

'I need your help with some shopping, beta.'

'I will be there soon.'

Kavya overheard our conversation and placed her hand on her hip as if she was about to yell.

'Why is Radhika's mom calling you so much suddenly?'

'I do not know! Maybe, she needs my help?'

'You should avoid going so frequently to her house, Vasu.'

'But why?'

'Come here!' Kavya signalled. She silently took out a pen and paper. She drew an intersecting venn diagram with two circles. On the left circle, she wrote "Radhika" and labelled it as "friend-zone". On the right, she wrote "Aunty". Then she drew a bigger circle covering the diagram.

I looked at what she was drawing and my eyes flickered. It was as if someone was trying to hypnotize me.

She looked at me and asked, 'Do you know the name of the bigger circle?'

I shook my head.

She wrote – *Bro-zoned!*

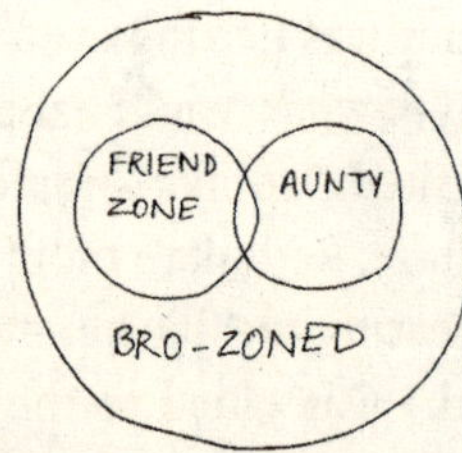

'You are moving from being "friend-zoned" to "bro-zoned", Vasu.'

Before I could say anything, my phone rang. Kavya looked at me with shock when I answered the call and left the room.

As soon I reached Radhika's home, she opened the door with a smile.

'You look joyful today, Radhika.'

'Mom was looking for you,' she said, almost blushing and went inside to call her mother. Aunty came out of her room and informed me that a few important guests were coming from Chandigarh. She handed me a list of snacks and two-thousand rupees.

I read the list which had some very specific instructions on it:

Two kg milk cake

One kg mewa ghewar

Six special Kesar lassi from Lassi wala

Dry fruit packets from the Laxmi Mishthan Bhandar at Johari Bazar road

I nodded, without caring to inquire about the need for such elaborate shopping. Then I asked Radhika, 'Are you ready?'

'Radhika will be busy. So could you please manage on your own?' her mom asked.

'Okay,' I said, still confused about the unknown occasion they were preparing to celebrate.

I was familiar with every shop in Jaipur. After an hour of making the purchases, I came back. Taking over the packets, Radhika's mother smiled at me and said, 'God bless you, beta!'

As I was enjoying her compliments, Radhika entered the room. She was dressed in a red suit and was glowing like the rising sun. For the first time, I saw her wearing a bindi. I was mesmerized by her magnificent face. She looked overdressed, but I refrained from questioning anything. Even though my heart was not ready to leave her house, I did eventually.

•

In the evening, Radhika and her mom came home with a packet of sweets. Radhika was still wearing the same red dress. She looked ethereal. It was a delight to see her radiant smile after so many days.

'Aunty, who came to your house?'

'Sanju's parents came from Chandigarh to meet us today,'

'But Sanju is in USA.'

'Yes, his parents came from Chandigarh to see Radhika,' Aunty said in a sparkling voice.

I shifted my gaze towards Radhika and she blushed.

This time I did not like her blushing face. Then, her mother dropped another atom bomb.

'Radhika's marriage is fixed. We are planning for a wedding in a few months.'

My eyes flickered. I wondered if I had heard them correctly. They were crystal clear, but I did not want to understand them.

'Is it a love marriage or arranged?' my mom asked.

'Love marriage. They studied together.'

I shifted a little and sat at the extreme corner. Their smiles, laughter and happy faces were piercing my heart.

The gregarious aunty came and offered the sweet which I had purchased from the market. I wished I had added some poison in it. Her mom was ecstatic as she put the milk cake in my mouth and said, 'Thank you, Vasu. You are a good brother.' Sluggishly I tried to gulp the tasteless sweet that was finding it hard to travel to my stomach.

I walked back to my room and closed the door gently. I sat on the bed and noticed a paper that was kept besides me. It had the diagram which Kavya had drawn earlier.

Radhika's mom had "bro-zoned" my love.

22

Black Dog

I retreated in my shell for a few days. I could not process the news of Radhika's marriage so I began avoiding her. Kavya tried to comfort me, but I assured her that I was fine.

I started spending more time at the office. Radhika's wedding was fixed for 12 November 2016. By now, I was more desperate for her to get married and go away from my life. While surfing on Instagram, I saw that Radhika had uploaded a few pictures with Sanju. She had even changed her status on Facebook from "single" to "in a relationship". I closed Instagram, but her picture lingered on in my mind. I opened Instagram again and looked at her genuine smile. I realized that nothing was more beautiful than a happy woman.

I avoided her WhatsApp messages and phone calls. Radhika had invited me a couple of times for dinner, but I refused, keeping myself busy at the hotel. I decided to vanish from the city as her wedding date came closer. I made an excuse for an official tour to Agra.

My mother was super excited about Radhika's wedding. She shared all the news related to her shopping, dresses, wedding hall booking, and house decorations with me. Papa had also started helping Radhika's family with the arrangements. It was like everyone was joining in to humiliate me.

I decided to leave the city, a day before Radhika's wedding. But my destiny had other plans. And Mr Modi had also cooked something against me.

On 8 November 2016, Prime Minister Narendra Modi delivered the demonetization speech that shocked India. The Indian government recalled the 500 and 1000 rupee notes. The immediate objective of demonetization was to flush out a large amount of black money hoarded in cash, and the long-term objective was to convert our cash-based economy into a digital one. All the cash transactions had stopped in the country. Everyone was in a bank queue to convert their cash. This added an extra burden on Kavya as a bank employee. She started coming home very late almost every day.

•

Two days before the wedding, Radhika and her mom came to our house. They went straight to mom and said, 'We need your help.'

Aunty discussed that they were short of cash for the wedding. Dad promised to provide all the possible help to them. Relieved, aunty moved to another room to discuss the details with my mother. Radhika was sitting with me on the sofa.

'How are you, Radhika?' I asked in a low voice.

'Why are you avoiding me?'

'Sorry, I have been busy with work.'

'You know I don't have many relatives. I really need my best friend on the most important day of my life.'

'Oh, but I am leaving for Agra tomorrow.'

'Oh! When will you be back?'

'After the wedding.'

'So, you will not be here for your best friend's wedding?'

I swallowed hard and shook my head.

'But I need my best friend.'

She looked at me for an answer, but I was tight-lipped. The emotionless face had conveyed the message.

'I understand. You have a job which you need to manage.'

'Sorry, Radhika. I am helpless.'

She sighed and said, 'So, you also left me in the end!'

Her words hit me. She tried to change the topic and asked, 'Pankaj is also getting married next week.'

'Pankaj, who?'

'The boy who was chosen to act as king in your place during our drama auditions in school. Remember?'

'Hmm. Are you in touch with him?'

'Yes, he just invited me on WhatsApp for the wedding.'

'Remember, you were selected as the queen. It must have been difficult to give up the lead role.'

'No, it was easy because you were not there. How could I participate as the queen if you couldn't be the king, Vasu?'

I gulped some air and everything flashed across my mind. How she had fought for me by withdrawing her name from the play. She was the only one who stood by me through thick and thin in school. She was the only one who never laughed at me. She was the only one who had walked back home with me everyday. We had so many memories together. She was the only friend I had!

'So, you are leaving tomorrow morning?' she asked.

I took a deep breath and said, 'No, I am not going anywhere. I was just joking.'

'What?' she asked angrily.

'How could I miss the moment when my princess becomes a queen?'

•

Mangal Kamana Guest House in Jaipur was booked for Radhika's wedding events. On the wedding day, she requested me to personally pick Sanju and his close relatives from the Jaipur airport. She said that it would make them happy as a close family member came to receive them.

I went to the airport to pick Sanju and his family. Jaipur airport was not only a place for me, it was a deep and profound emotion. I stood there, controlling my overwhelming emotions and wearing a fake smile. I was holding a placard, which said:

Radhika weds Sanju

Team Bride Welcomes You

•

On the wedding day, I stayed at the office and returned home late in the night. I received a couple of calls from Radhika, but I did not answer them. Mom and dad had already left for the wedding venue. Kavya and I were the only ones at home. My phone rang again. The call was from an unknown number.

'Where are you?' Radhika asked as soon as I picked up the call.

'In the office.'

'Are you crazy, Vasu? Today is my wedding. Why are you not answering my phone?'

'Sorry. I was busy at work.'

'Please come fast. Everyone is asking about you.'

I disconnected the call and dumped the phone on the bed. Kavya was hearing the conversation.

'Are you seriously going to her wedding, Vasu?' Kavya asked.

I nodded.

'Why? It will not be easy.'

'I always wanted to see her in a wedding dress, Kavya.'

Kavya rolled her eyes and let out a frustrating sigh. She kept a hand on my shoulder and patted silently. We quickly got dressed and left for the wedding venue. I drove the car in silence.

'Are you okay?' Kavya asked twice during the drive.

'I'm fine.' I was on the brink of tears, but I maintained my composure.

We reached the resort and met a few relatives. It was a small wedding with very few guests. Kavya went inside to see Radhika. I was feeling uneasy, so I sat in the last row. I could hear the conversation of well-dressed ladies.

One of them said, 'The arrangements are not that good.'

'Might be the demonetization effect,' said the other women.

'All these are unnecessary excuses to save money. They could have gone for a more lavish wedding. After all, the boy is an NRI.'

I smirked at their strange conversation.

I closed my lips and gazed at the ground. Slowly the ambience changed into a more festive mood. I saw the camera guy placing the camera stand at two different angles. The music changed from party to instrumental melody. Few of the guests were busy eating dinner. The rare dream of seeing my Radhika in a bridal dress was about to come true.

Finally, Radhika entered the hall. She walked towards the stage, escorted by two girls. All the eyes were set on her. A few enthusiastic relatives were showering flowers on her. I wondered where these people were when her father was struggling in the hospital.

I gazed at my Radhika's face. She was looking breathtakingly gorgeous. It was the moment I had dreamt of all my life, but not this way. I clenched my teeth, made a fist and took a few long breaths. My eyes flickered and I started panting.

'She is so beautiful,' a female voice spoke.

'Both the bride and groom are perfect,' another aunty said.

I closed my eyes, exhaled, and rushed out. After walking for a few kilometres, I reached a liquor shop.

'Which is the most expensive brand you have?' I asked.

'Jonny Walker, Teachers and Black Dog.'

'One Black Dog!'

I also bought a few plastic glasses, ice, snacks and strode towards the open parking. I was mixing ice, water and whiskey when my phone rang. I didn't pick up the call, but it rang again. I answered the call after the third attempt, 'Yes, Kavya!'

'Where are you, Vasu?'

'I didn't want to stay there.'

'Okay, I will come to you. Where are you?'

'I am in the parking area.'

I disconnected the call. As soon as I had finished the first peg, Kavya found me.

'I knew it!' she said angrily.

I closed my eyes and looked down. She said, 'Bro, you are a brave boy.'

'Didi, I don't have the strength to see all this. Please don't push me.'

'I am not here to push you. I just came here wondering, how can you drink alone?' she said with a smile.

'It's my pain and I need to manage it alone.'

'No, it's *our* pain.'

I pulled out another plastic glass. I mixed the drink, water and ice cubes.

She asked, looking at the bottle, 'Black Dog? Why such an expensive whiskey?'

I lifted the glass and said, 'No one wants a black dog. Everyone wants the white one. So, I thought at least I deserve a Black Dog.'

'But I don't care if it is black, white or grey. I love *this* dog.'

I faked a smile as a tear rolled down my cheeks.

We raised the glasses and shouted, 'Cheers!'

23

The Parting Tears

That night, I slept peacefully. Whiskey had made sure that I forget everything for a few hours. Or perhaps, it had helped me not to cry.

I woke up at 9 a.m. and found the house to be empty. I walked to the kitchen and made lemonade in lukewarm water. I had a few sips and soon, I felt relieved from the painful hangover. Kavya had gone to the bank, and mom must have been with Radhika's family to bid goodbye to her as she was leaving for Chandigarh.

I sat on the sofa and switched on the TV, trying to distract myself. But still, Radhika kept running in my mind. I turned off the TV and went to our temple in the corner. I looked at all the idols and my eyes landed on Krishna, who was standing with Radha. I was filled with tears.

I resumed on the sofa and checked my phone. There were seven missed calls and a few messages. I switched off the phone and made one more lemon drink for myself.

Suddenly, someone rang the doorbell, but I did not move. If it were my parents, they had the keys and I was not interested to see anyone else. The bell rang again. I sulked and rushed to answer but did not unlock the bolt. Unknown fear ran through me.

'Vassooooo!' I shuddered upon hearing Radhika's voice

I did not open the door. She screamed again, 'Vassoooo! I am leaving.'

Unable to resist my temptation to avoid her, I opened the door. There she was, dressed in a heavy, bright salwar suit. She was standing there with Hunk who was wagging his tail.

'Why did you not come to the stage, Vasu? I don't have any picture with you.'

I remained tight-lipped.

'I am leaving for Chandigarh. Please take care of Hunk.'

I nodded. She seemed to be in a hurry.

'Vasu, I always cursed my luck because of my father, but then, god gifted me a friend like you. Now I have no complaints.'

I smiled slightly and she hugged me. This might be the last time I was seeing my Radhika.

She whispered, 'Thanks, Vasu. Never change, my boy.'

I tied Hunk in the room and went to see her off. I met Sanju and we shook hands.

Before leaving, he said, 'Thank you for taking care of my Radhika.'

I stood there as my life moved away from me.

Mom mumbled, 'She is a lucky girl. She has everything in life.'

And my mind whispered, 'Yes, Radhika. Suddenly you have everything, and I lost everything.'

24

The Slap

India finally came out of its demonetization phase. The Indian government had launched the new two-thousand rupee note. Everyone was gradually shifting to digital transactions.

Radhika went to Bhutan for her honeymoon. She shared her honeymoon pictures with me on WhatsApp. I didn't reply to her, nor did I ask her to share more pictures. I had never even bothered to ask whether she was happy or not. Probably, it was my lack of enthusiasm that made her stop sharing the pictures with me after a while. Gradually, I got into the habit of smoking and it became an integral part of my daily routine.

Once, during the break, I walked to the office smoking area and saw that my colleague, Usha was also there. I took out my cigarette and then realised that I had left the lighter in my cabin. Usha understood and offered me her lighter. I took it gratefully and drew a satisfactory puff.

'How are you, Vasu?'

I shrugged, noncommittally.

'You don't seem to be doing well.'

'What made you think that, Usha?'

'You did not smoke before. But now, you are here during every break. Even more than me!'

'You think I am upset just because I am smoking more than you?'

'Yes, and also because I am not the one who is listening to sad songs all the time.'

I took a deep puff, releasing my stress in the form of smoke.

'I need a favour, Vasu.'

I nodded.

'I have a planned leave for three days. Could you please take over my duties?'

'But that is not my department. You work at the front desk.'

'We have the same manager, so I will explain everything to you.'

'But why me? Isn't there somebody else?'

'Because you are my friend, Vasu.'

I stopped smoking. Suddenly, I found the room to be very suffocating. The word "friend" had triggered some memories.

'Fine, I will help.'

'Thank you.'

Usha had written a formal email that in her absence, I would officially take charge of the front desk activities. She had explained everything related to the job to me. I supported the front desk team for two days. I understood the intricacies of managing customer expectations. It was far more difficult than event management.

It is only when we slip into the shoes of another person that we realize that others have more sores on their feet than us.

•

A group of twenty-seven German tourists had arrived to explore Rajasthan. They had booked almost half of the hotel rooms. The top management was excited about their arrival and the sales head was coming to examine the arrangements.

As he entered the lobby, everyone became quiet. He was dressed in a heavy coat. He paced up and down the lobby and then, came to the reception and shouted, 'Why is the air conditioner temperature so high? It should be between 21 to 23 degrees Celsius.'

He waved his hand and signalled at a staff member who ran to fix the temperature.

As soon as one of the German guests entered the lobby, he wore a smile. He adjusted his coat and hair and approached the German lady, 'Ma'am, how long will you be staying here?'

She did not reply. Then, he questioned again, 'How long will you be staying?'

'Sir, she doesn't know English,' I reasoned.

The sales head passed a nasty look at me. He locked his lips inward, and asked, 'Who are you?'

'Sir, I am Vasu, working here as an event manager.'

'What are you doing here at the front desk?'

'I am the temporary substitute for the front desk duty,' I replied.

'But the front desk role is exclusively for female staff members.'

'Almost all the women staff members are on leave till tomorrow.'

'Where is the manager?' he roared.

'Let me check, sir,' I said and shivered.

The manager understood that he was going to have a bad day. He came running to the lobby and greeted the sales head with a smile.

'Why is *he* managing the front desk?'

'Sir, all the female staff members are on urgent leave.'

The sales head scanned me from top to bottom and said, 'Why have you selected him then? Couldn't you have chosen a smart guy?'

I was busy allocating rooms to the guests when his words hit me. I stopped my work for a few seconds. I was struggling hard to control myself. I even had a glass of water to calm myself down.

The manager came and said, 'Vasu, hand over the charge of front desk to Rohan.'

'No, I will not,' I raised my voice.

The sales head neared and mumbled, 'Don't create a scene in front of the guests.'

'I want to talk to you in private,' I said in a low voice.

'No, you can write an email,' he answered sternly.

'I want to talk to you in private.' I raised my voice. The German guest could sense the tension in the air. She shifted a few steps back.

The sales head flushed and guided me to a backside room.

He walked in and roared in frustration, 'What do you want to talk to me about?'

'Why do you think I am not smart enough to handle the desk?'

'I don't want to talk to you about this.'

'Is it because I am dark, and you are fair?'

'I said no discussion on this or else you will lose your job.'

I laughed.

'You are good-looking because you have fair skin?'

'Yes! Now, get back to work.'

I gritted my teeth and closed my eyes. I slapped him thrice and shouted, 'It was a pleasure working with you, sir.'

I was panting as I left the place. I went outside and lit my cigarette. As I was about to finish my cigarette, my phone vibrated. My manager had sent me a message:

I had never seen this side of your personality. I am impressed by how you took a stand for yourself today. Well done, Vasu. We will miss you in the workplace.

Take care.

25

The Transformation

Kavya Speaks

We could not believe that Vasu had slapped his senior manager at his workplace. When I got to know about the incident, I was happy. Finally, Vasu had shown some audacity in life. But at the same time, I was also missing my innocent Vasu. The brother, who would pester me with stupid questions. The man, who never took anything to heart for long and would forget everything soon.

Vasu had stopped sharing his feelings with me. I knew I was the only one he talked to about Radhika, but we don't talk anymore about her. His pain was so intense that he even changed his office route, trying to avoid even a glimpse of Radhika's house. However, he occasionally visited her mom. I regretted the fact that Radhika lived in our locality. It seemed that everything reminded Vasu of her.

Radhika was looking amazing in her honeymoon pictures from Bhutan and Chandigarh. I guess she was happy in her life. I often replied and appreciated Radhika on her WhatsApp profile pictures and she too would always reply to me.

I confess that sometimes, I would get jealous of her. She was so average in studies. Even though she is four years younger than me, she got her perfect wedding.

Six families have rejected me so far. They came to see me, but later, they made excuses about my horoscope, job or some other trivial issue. I know the reality and I guess, everyone else does too. They needed a beautiful face, which was not me.

•

One night, Radhika posted a beautifully clicked picture from Pinjore Gardens. However, something did not feel right. She was not looking her radiant self; the serenity was missing from her face. I complimented her in a comment. She acknowledged and asked about how Vasu was doing. I understood that Vasu had stopped replying to Radhika. But I had often seen him scanning her pictures on Instagram. My missing cigarettes were an indication that he was still getting over her. The name "Radhika" did not bring a smile to his face anymore.

I missed the Vasu who would smile at my silly jokes, even when they were not funny. I missed the times when he would come to me to seek my guidance on his love life. I missed the Vasu who would go to the temple once in a week. I missed the guy who watched *Kung Fu Panda* even when he grew up and laughed out loud like an innocent kid. I missed my smiling brother who had shiny white teeth. I regretted the fact that I filled his head with so many dreams. In his journey to fulfil them, he had lost himself somewhere along the way.

One day he asked me, 'Why did Krishna never marry Radha?' I was surprised by his question.

After taking a deep breath, I said, 'Krishna never married Radha because Radha finally realized that he was not an ordinary being. She loved him immensely, but in a way that a devotee loves god. Her love for Krishna was beyond physical pleasure. It was not lust, rather it was pure, deep and divine. Therefore, the question of marriage completely disappeared from the picture.'

I wondered why Vasu related with Krishna and Radha so much. We are humans and we are imperfect, but we are perfect in our own unique ways. I was anxious to break the illusion. Or else, he would start living the life of a destitute.

To live like Radha, someone should have Krishna in their life.

26

Pure Love

Life's two biggest curses are free time and a bad experience that haunts you. Now that I had no office to go to, my mind was preoccupied with the thoughts of the past. The memories made me miserable, so I decided to do something productive. My manager had given me a glowing recommendation, so I started exploring more job opportunities in the hospitality industry.

To get started, I made an impressive resume, seeking Kavya's help. Once I was ready, I uploaded my details on job hunting sites. I even created a LinkedIn profile to broaden my professional network. Even though it was a slow process, it was gratifying to see how I was investing in my skills. Slowly, I started getting interview calls.

Once, while I was surfing through my LinkedIn profile, mom announced, 'Radhika is four years younger than Kavya.'

Dad shifted his gaze and pretended to read the newspaper. However, it was understood that he was the target. I decided to focus on my work.

'Seems like the newspaper is more important than your family.' Mom took the second shot. The intensity and voice modulation hinted that the drama was about to begin.

'What can I do?' dad retorted.

'You can go out and search for a suitable boy.'

'We are trying our best. Please be patient!'

After a short and intense argument, they stopped talking and looked at me. I silently sat in a corner, trying to eat my breakfast.

My mom whispered, 'Vasu is also getting older now. We need to settle him down as well.'

I was surprised by her statement, but chose to remain quiet. Mom had become restless after Radhika's wedding.

'What happened to you? Why didn't you go to the office today?' she asked suddenly, staring at me.

'I left the job,' I answered, without looking at her.

'What will you do then?'

'I have applied to a few good companies. If I don't get an exciting opportunity, I will support dad in his business.' There was a smile on my father's face.

'But you could have waited till your marriage.'

'Why?' I asked, irritated.

'A person with a stable job is always preferred over someone who is struggling in a business.'

I did not want to discuss this further, so I decided to go out.

'I am going to the salon,' I screamed.

'Wait!' She went inside and came out with an umbrella and said, 'Please carry this.'

'But there is no possibility of rain today.'

'This is to save you from sunburn.'

I sniggered and picked the umbrella. Then, mumbled, 'No one can burn me more now.'

I went to the salon and asked for a shave. I sat on the comfortable chair and closed my eyes. The staff started applying the shaving cream. All I could do was to think about Kavya. I had never tried asking how she felt about all the rejections she was facing. After the shaving service, I left and rode through the nearby streets. I wanted to avoid going home. It seemed a lot had changed around the neighbourhood. Many new shops had opened in the locality and a few old ones had shut down as well.

I walked aimlessly on the same old path. I had crossed Shyam lassi, a tea stall, few food joints, and reached the temple finally. I had no desire to visit the temple anymore, but I wondered how I had ended up there. There were only a few women at the gate. I decided to walk in. Radha and Krishna were smiling in the temple. Krishna was playing the flute. I wondered why I have never seen Krishna without his flute. I bowed my head and prayed for my sister's wedding.

When I finished the prayer, my attention was diverted to a man who was sitting at the corner. The old man had decorated his forehead with the longest sandalwood *tilak* that I had ever seen. He was delivering a lecture to a few middle-aged and elderly women with a pleasant smile. I looked at him. I wondered why mostly women participated in such things.

I was about to cross him and step outside the temple when suddenly he chanted, 'Radha! Radha!' The word "Radha" captured my attention. I decided to spend some time listening to the man.

'We usually remember the eighth avatar of Vishnu as the little butter thief, or as the charioteer-guide of Arjun in the *Mahabharata* who helped the warrior to find his path during the battle. However, Krishna was much more than that. He was a disciple, a guru, a cowherd and a messenger. Throughout his life, Krishna enacted so many roles.'

I raised my hand and he nodded his bald decorated head at me.

'What happened to Radha when Krishna left?'

Few women threw an unwanted look to my side. The bald man passed a smile and explained, 'According to the Vedas, lord Krishna fell in love with Radha when he was just eight years old. His affection for her was so true and pure that he maintained his feelings throughout his lifetime. It is believed that lord Krishna loved his flute as much as he loved Radha. It was his musical talents which attracted Radha towards him. Therefore, he kept his flute with him all the time. But, Radha and Krishna could not be together.

'Radha married someone else. During old age, after retiring from all the duties, she went to meet her Krishna for the last time. When she reached Dwarka, she heard about Krishna's marriage to Rukmini and Satyabhama, but she did not feel sad.

'When Krishna saw Radha, he was elated. However, nobody knew Radha in Dwarka. She lived in the palace, but she could not feel the spiritual connection with lord Krishna like before. Therefore, she decided to go away from the palace. Radha did not know where she was going. She was lonely and weak in her last days.

'Lord Krishna came to her. He asked her to make a wish which he could fulfil, but Radha refused. When he requested again, Radha said that she wanted to see him playing the flute for one last time. Krishna started playing a harmonious tune, and she took her last breath.

'Radha's soul left her body while listening to the tunes of the flute. Lord Krishna could not bear the grief of Radha's death. He broke his flute as a symbolic end of their love and threw it into the bush. After that, he did not play the flute ever again.'

27

Set Me Free

I lay on the bed, my eyes glued to the ceiling. My mind was lost, wondering about Radha and Krishna. I never thought Krishna had lived such a painful life. I had always seen him dancing and smiling in images, movies and serials. His biological mother lived in jail for years and he could not marry his beloved Radha.

My mobile phone vibrated with a notification.

Hey Vasu, how are you?

Radhika had dropped a message on WhatsApp. I read and wondered what to reply, but ignored it. I kept the phone in one corner. It vibrated again and this time it said: *Hope you are doing well.*

I checked the time. It was 12:42 a.m. She had never pinged me so late. I took a long breath and decided to reply.

Hi Radhika, how are you?

I am doing good, Vasu. Where will you be tomorrow?

I am here in Jaipur only.

I am coming to Jaipur, Vasu.

Okay Good!

Can you send someone to the airport? I don't want to put unnecessary burden on mom.

I am busy Radhika, else I would have come to receive you. But I will send a taxi.

Thanks, Vasu.

I kept the phone aside and closed my eyes. I smiled as I was going to meet her after a long time. But I wanted to avoid her presence with Sanju. So, I called Mahesh.

'Can you go to Jaipur domestic airport tomorrow at 5 p.m.?'

'Sure bhaiya,' the driver said. 'But I have a CNG vehicle. Hope there is no big luggage?'

'Oh, let me check.'

I pinged Radhika again.

Hey Radhika, how much luggage would you be carrying?

Just one bag. I am coming alone.

I am coming alone.

I read that line thrice.

The next day, I reached the airport well before time to receive her. I looked at the other taxi drivers. Most of them were holding a placard with the name of their guest. So, I picked a white sheet and wrote: WELCOME RADHIKA.

I read the placard twice and felt something was missing. I thought for a few minutes and edited the line to: WELCOME MRS RADHIKA.

After desperately waiting for more than twenty minutes, I saw her. She was wearing a white t-shirt and body fitting jeans. She was looking lovely as ever. She had her hair curled and wrapped in a neat bun. She looked totally different yet strikingly beautiful with her red lipstick and tiny sindoor on her forehead. She was holding a fashionable leather bag and her big black shades were hiding almost half of her face.

She walked towards me and we saw each other. There was a smile on my face. When she removed the shades, our eyes met. My lips moved to say, 'Welcome Mrs Radhika' but instead, I showed her the placard. She nudged my right shoulder and smiled. We exchanged a half hug, or rather, an awkward hug.

As soon as she sat in the car, she said, 'I knew you would come to receive me.'

'How were you so sure about that?' I turned on the engine and shifted the gear.

'Because you did not share the taxi driver's number.'

'Seems I am bad at planning things.'

'You are the best, Vasu. Always there for me.'

'How is Sanju?'

'He is good, but let's not talk about him or any relatives. Let's talk about something good.'

'Okay! Do you want to eat something?'

'No! But let's go to Hawa Mahal.'

'You don't want to go home? You must be tired.'

'No, I am good.'

Why did she want to see Hawa Mahal suddenly? Why did she not want to talk about Sanju or his family?

My mind was abuzz with questions.

We reached Hawa Mahal in half an hour. With a history of over two hundred years, Hawa Mahal is perhaps the most iconic monument in Jaipur. What makes this palace one of the top attractions for travellers is its unique architecture that comprises 953 windows. We walked and explored all the corners of this historical place. It was crowded with foreigners and Indian tourists. We walked until the end and Radhika opened one of the windows. We were able to see the glittering Jaipur streets below.

'You know why these windows were made?' she asked.

'Yes, during those days, the purdah system was strictly followed, and royal women weren't allowed to show their faces to strangers or even appear in public. The palace had these windows, which enabled them to get a glimpse of the day-to-day activities and festivities happening on the street below.'

'Can you imagine the life of those women, Vasu?'

'Yes, those were rich and respected ladies.'

'Those respected ladies had all the luxury, but no freedom.'

I pursed my lips and tried to read her face. It was obvious that she was facing some trouble in life. I wanted to ask so many things and wondered where to start. We sat there until dusk.

I decided to divert her mind and suggested, 'Let's have your favourite samosa from Shankar Masala Chowk.'

'I don't feel like eating anything.'

'Let's go for a drink.'

'No! I have stopped drinking, Vasu.'

'Okay, but why?'

'Because, I am pregnant.'

I was blank for a few seconds.

'Congratulations!' I said, finally gathering my emotions.

'No need, Vasu.'

'What happened, Radhika?'

'Nothing.' She shifted her gaze.

'Are you not happy with Sanju?'

She looked down and flushed, 'I loved the Sanju whom I met in Jaipur, but after staying in the USA, he started taking me for granted. He has serious temperament issues. He is not the same person anymore. He treats me like a slave and I am not allowed to do anything without his permission.'

'Don't lose hope,' I said.

'Hope is a fool's paradise, Vasu.'

I did not know what to say.

'But why are you suddenly back here, Radhika?'

'He slapped me last night.'

28
Birthday Boy

It was a chilly day in January 2018. The censor had board banned the film *Padmaavat* which had created a lot of controversy in Rajasthan. But, it was also turning out to be a boon for tourism in the state. Plenty of tourists from across the country had been flocking to the significant cities of the region, which included Udaipur and Chittorgarh.

Papa advised opening a branch in Chittorgarh to tap into the flourishing business. He had a detailed plan to cover Chittorgarh, Udaipur and Kumbhalgarh. As many big and organized tourist players were active in the city, it was tough doing business in Jaipur only.

'When do you plan to go to Chittorgarh?' dad asked while scanning the recent booking lists.

'I am thinking of starting the Chittorgarh business as soon as possible.'

'But why so suddenly?' he asked.

'There is a huge rush to visit the place. It seems the *Padmaavat* controversy is doing great for tourism. I also want to do some research before making any investment.'

Papa nodded. He always spends time with us. He never denied any request for money and had never forced any decisions on me.

I called Radhika in the evening to go for a walk. She refused initially, but after insisting, she joined me. It had been so long since we interacted with each other like this.

'What happened, Radhika? Why are you so quiet?'

'No, I'm fine. I may take a few days to become better.'

'Okay, what are you doing the day after tomorrow?'

'Why? Anything special, Vasu?'

'It is my birthday.'

She smiled. 'Wow! I completely forgot!'

'So, are you free?'

'Yes, I am.'

'Let's celebrate together.'

'I want to avoid going to any public gatherings. Hope you can understand.'

'No fancy stuff. Just a simple dinner.'

'Perfect.'

•

It was my twenty-fifth birthday. I was waiting for my phone to vibrate at midnight, but I did not receive a birthday wish from her. I checked her "last seen" status on WhatsApp which was at 11 p.m. I assumed she might have slept.

Kavya said, 'Stop expecting things from her now.'

I gave her a hard stare and my lower lip puffed up.

'Happy birthday, lover boy!'

Kavya bellowed and pulled out the Sula red wine and said, 'Just because you can't dance, doesn't mean you should not dance.'

We raised the toast and after a few sips, I picked up my phone to check for any notifications. I restarted the phone, assuming that there might be some technical glitch.

'She is a married woman, Vasu,' Kavya said. I flushed and flared my nostrils.

The next morning, I got calls from mamaji, chacha ji and other relatives, but not Radhika. She did not even drop any messages. I checked her Instagram story and I smiled. There, on her Instagram story, she had put a picture of us with a caption – *Happy birthday, my best friend.*

I felt awkward that she remembered my birthday, but did not call even once.

Is she not well? Or was I expecting too much from Mrs Radhika?

Mom presented a small packet of sweets and instructed, 'Vasu, today is your birthday. Please visit Radhika's mom. Give these sweets and take her blessings.'

How could I turn down any opportunity to meet Radhika?

Hunk was looking at me with innocent eyes. I guessed he wanted to come with me too. I took Hunk along and walked out with the sweet box. When I reached her place, I rang the bell.

'Hey, Vasu! Happy birthday, how are you?' Her mom said as soon as she opened the door.

'Thanks, I am good, aunty. Mom has sent some sweets for you.'

She invited me inside the house. I sat on the sofa and was busy playing with Hunk. Radhika's mom came with a glass of water and sweets in a tray.

'Where is Radhika?'

'She went back to Chandigarh. She has left a note for you.' Radhika's mom gave me a folded piece of paper.

I took the paper and asked, 'But why did she go back so suddenly?'

'Sanju came yesterday and they decided to fly back last night.'

'Oh!'

'They will be shifting to USA soon, Vasu,' aunty said, beaming with joy.

I did not touch the sweets offered by aunty and opened the letter.

Happy birthday, Vasu. Sorry, I am leaving for Chandigarh on such a short notice. Hope you can understand my situation. Few remain silent to save a relationship and many relationships break because someone chooses silence.

Thanks for always being there for me.

29

Most Cherished Gift

A family was coming to see Kavya on Sunday. He was the seventh boy who was coming to 'see' her. Every time someone came, it changed the atmosphere at home. Mom started shouting more. Dad stopped speaking. Kavya gulped more alcohol.

With the negative environment around and dying business in Jaipur, I had pushed myself more for temporary relocation to Chittorgarh. I felt bad for Kavya as she did not have such options. In the evening, I talked to Kavya.

'Kavya, someone is coming to see you.'

'Yes, but that is not your business.'

'Why would you say that?'

'Because you are leaving for Chittorgarh.'

'I will be coming home twice a month.'

'Twice in a month?' she smirked.

'Show me the picture of the boy.'

'He is not handsome,' Kavya said, handing me her phone.

'Who cares?' I said and jumped on her bed. I grabbed the phone and checked the boy's profile on Facebook. I browsed through his pictures. He had received only a few comments.

'Are you sure about him?' I asked.

'I told you, he is not handsome.'

'But you deserve a good person.'

'Vasu, everyone wants a good-looking partner. I am four years elder than your Radhika and yet, I am unmarried.'

I closed my mouth and merely nodded. Her answer told me not to ask anything further.

'But why are you leaving Jaipur now, Vasu? You can always go later.'

'This is related to work. We cannot delay.'

'It's related to *her*. I know.'

'No, it is not related to Radhika.'

Kavya continued to stare at me for a few seconds.

I took a deep breath and shifted to my bed. I tried watching TV, but Kavya's mind seemed to be stuck somewhere else. She looked at me twice and then asked, 'Why are you so nice to her? Why is she so important to you?'

'Seriously, you need an answer?'

'Yes, but do not give me the stupid answer that you love her.'

I sighed and said, 'She is the only one who never made me feel unworthy. When no one sat next to me in school, she did. She denied becoming the queen in the school play when I could not be the king because of my looks. She fought for me when I was insulted in the class. She is the only friend with whom I can share anything without hesitation. She is the only person whom I know beyond my family. She never made me feel that I am a below-average looking boy.'

I started panting.

'But you never told her that you love her,' Kavya said.

'I wish I could tell her, but it does not matter anymore,' I said in a feeble voice.

'You are holding on to something for so long.'

'I am not holding on to anything, Kavya.'

She left her bed and picked her bulky, ceramic cup and handed it over to me.

'What am I supposed to do with this empty cup?'

'It looks like an empty cup, but it carries some weight, Vasu.'

'It is not very heavy.'

'Hmm, can you hold this for a few seconds?'

'Yes, I can.'

'Can you hold this for a few minutes?'

'Yes, I can manage, Kavya.'

'Can you hold this for a few hours?'

I shook my head.

'If you hold it for longer, you will get a sprain.'

'Why would I hold the cup for so long?'

'Exactly, Vasu! Do not hold on to her memories in your heart. The longer you will wait for Radhika, the deeper pain you will feel.'

I leaned into a sloping position on the bed. I had lost the argument but then, I mumbled, 'Do not compare a lifeless ceramic cup with my best friend.'

•

The next morning, I kept my luggage in the car, ready to leave for Chittorgarh. Mom was sad but dad was puffed with pride. Only Kavya was teary-eyed.

For the first time, I was going outside Jaipur to live on my own. Earlier, the travel business was majorly focused on Delhi, Agra and Jaipur. We had now decided to expand to other cities like Jodhpur, Udaipur and Chittorgarh. We were also in partnership with the travel giant, Expedia. All the Rajasthan bookings for them were managed by us.

I played a critical role in the expansion of our business. With my previous hotel management experience, relationship-building skills and tech-savvy approach, we were making rapid progress.

It was hard to deal with taxi drivers. Most of them hailed from Uttar Pradesh, Bihar and West Bengal. Quite often they went to their home town and surprisingly, they never returned to their job. I wondered how dad was managing the taxi and tour business.

It had been a few months since my arrival in Chittorgarh. When mom called me up, she informed me that Kavya's marriage meeting had gone well.

One day, Kavya called me to share the good news. Her marriage was fixed. Her voice indicated that she was thrilled. I decided to visit home the following week.

I was all set to leave for Jaipur and had almost packed my stuff. I did not inform anyone as I wanted to surprise them. I had barely started for home when I received a message from Kavya.

I have news.

Good or bad? I checked.

That you need to decide. Your Radhika is blessed with a baby girl.

I took a long breath, switched on the AC, and sat there for a few minutes. Then I cancelled the travel plan to Jaipur.

•

Kavya's wedding functions were scheduled in April and I decided to be home in March.

The wedding was arranged in a big banquet hall. Anyone could have noticed the difference between Kavya and Radhika's weddings. There were fewer people for selfies. Only a few aunties talked about how gorgeous the couple looked. I remember one lady saying, 'He must be good at heart.'

While everyone was delighted about Kavya getting married, I wondered what it would be like without her at home. There would be no one to guide me anymore. Who would sit with me and drink at night? Who would draw stupid lines and diagrams on paper and behave like the most intelligent girl on earth? Who would make me believe that I had not lost everything?

An hour before Kavya's *vidaai* with her groom, I was sitting silently in the room. She was busy exchanging pleasantries with other relatives.

'Hey Vasu, come here!' Kavya had suddenly barged into the room.

She handed me the key to her scooty and said, 'Self-start is not working, so get it repaired.'

She then opened the almirah. 'It is empty now. You can keep your clothes here. And now, you can sleep on my king-size bed too.'

She wrote something on a piece of paper and said, '"Love_Vasu" is the laptop's password.'

Suddenly, I realized there will be no one to fight for the laptop, and there will be no one to throw me off the king-size bed. I could use the entire room, and everything was mine – TV, almirah, laptop, scooty, books and her memories. I realized that I did not want any of those. Instead, I wanted my sister.

'Why do we get married didi?'

'Don't call me didi.'

'Didi, you are also leaving me.'

She sat on the bed and tears started rolling down her cheeks. We did not speak for a few seconds. Mom shouted, 'Kavya, come! The car is here.'

Kavya mumbled, 'I need to leave, Vasu.'

I nodded.

'Say something.'

I smiled, but could not find the right words to express myself. I picked up the scooty key and kept it in the almirah. I turned to face her and said, 'This almirah, the scooty key, the king-size bed and the table – everything in this house will always belong to my didi.'

She covered her face and started sobbing. I sat near her and put a hand around her shoulder. 'Whenever I had a feeling that I had lost everything, I had my sister. I was stupid enough to never value such a cherished gift. I was busy chasing the fool's paradise.'

Panting, with a running nose, I said, 'I don't want anything, I just want my didi. Please don't go.'

She gulped and shook her head in denial.

'Can I hug my didi?' I asked.

She hugged me and whispered, 'Love you, my lover boy. Remember, you are the most handsome boy I have ever known.'

30

Tanya

From that day onwards, I never called Kavya by her name. I started calling her Kavya didi. Now I had enough reasons to leave the city. There was neither didi at home, nor Radhika in the locality.

Soon I shifted to Udaipur and kept relocating to different places in the name of business expansion. I called mom every alternate day and she shared the gossip of the entire universe. This time around, she had updated me that Radhika's mom had developed an infection in her kidney. Once in a month, she had to go for dialysis. Her blood pressure was irregular and often high.

Radhika had told me to take care of her mother, but I was not there when she needed me the most. I checked with Radhika on WhatsApp and noticed that she had dropped a message around six months back. I checked her Facebook, Instagram and WhatsApp. She had not posted anything anywhere recently. Her last post on Instagram was also six months old. It looked like she had suddenly vanished from the world.

I stalked her Instagram profile and looked at her picture with her mother. Radhika was smiling at her. I noticed that I had missed home for more than six months. I kept the phone aside and wondered when was the last time I hugged my mom. Suddenly I felt homesick. I decided to not delay any further and visit my home town. Upon seeing me, my mother scolded, 'Why did you come home? You should have stayed back there only, rather than being with your old mom.' However, she melted into my hug.

Later, mom updated me how mamaji and chachaji's kids were doing great in their studies.

'Wow, what are they doing?'

She went on a marathon of appreciation for two minutes. I shook my head and shrugged my shoulder. I wanted to say "who cares" but she did.

Suddenly she said, 'Radhika is also struggling.' I stiffened upon hearing it.

'What happened to Radhika?'

'Her mom is on dialysis. She has to go with her once in a month. There seems to be some problem with her husband too.'

I sat on the sofa and gazed down. I confessed to myself that I did not feel bad for her. Something was dying within me and I had begun to change.

•

I went to meet Radhika's mother that evening. She opened the door and welcomed me with a smile. Her complexion had turned pale and she had more grey hair than before. She went to fetch a soft drink for me. I noticed her unclean and unorganized home. I concluded that she hardly had any visitors.

She served a soft drink and we spoke about my work, life and everything. Seeing her condition, I felt guilty about not being there.

'Are you here till Monday?'

'Yes, what happened, aunty?

'Radhika is coming here on Monday. Could you help her?'

'Is she coming alone?'

'Oh! You are not aware?'

'Aware of what?'

'She got divorced a few days back. She is relocating back to Jaipur.'

I was startled.

Every pain has some pleasure hidden in it. Every pleasure is some pain in disguise. We may stick to only black or white, but reality remains in the shades of grey.

'Don't worry aunty. I will pick her up from the airport.'

'Thanks, Vasu. You are a true brother.'

•

When I went to receive Radhika, she spotted me from a distance and passed a feeble smile. She walked out, carrying three big suitcases on a trolley, and held her daughter.

Radhika was dressed in a short denim skirt and white top. She had her hair tied up in a ponytail. This version of Radhika was completely different from the one I had picked up the last time. Her makeup was much brighter, and her face was glowing. The top was deep enough that could distract me from seeing her face. She was becoming more glamorous with age. I gazed at the cute little angel that clung to her. For the first time, I was seeing a more beautiful face than Radhika's.

I did not ask how she was and thought to talk about something better.

'She is so sweet. What is her name?'

'You should ask her,' Radhika said, pointing at the baby girl.

'What your name?' I asked looking at her.

'Tanya,' she replied in a sweet voice.

'How old is she?'

'Thirteen months.'

I took the heavy luggage from Radhika. It seemed she had packed the entire house. The car trunk barely managed to accommodate the luggage and the rest was dropped on the back seat of the car. Radhika sat in the front passenger seat with me while Tanya sat in the back seat, playing with her mom's phone.

'What is the plan now, Radhika?'

'No plan.' She opened her purse and pulled out a cigarette. She lit it with a heavy metal lighter. Taking the first puff, she said, 'I have stopped planning my life anymore.'

'But you have a daughter.'

'One of the most important rights under divorce and matrimonial laws is the right to claim maintenance. I got a decent amount on the ground of alimony.'

There was confidence in her. I wondered how she had managed the court case alone.

'Oh! How much did you get in the name of alimony?'

'I got twenty-five lakhs for separation and shall receive twenty-five thousand every month for Tanya's education.'

My jaw dropped. I realized that she was so expensive to maintain.

She dragged a puff and said, 'If the woman is not earning, the court will consider the woman's age, her educational qualifications and her ability to earn, to decide the amount of the alimony. All Indian laws are made to help women.'

'You have learned so much about law!'

She shrugged and puffed at her cigarette. Then, she whispered, 'I will enjoy my life and take care of my mother. I might marry again.'

'You want to marry again?'

She folded her legs on the seat and I could see her bare white thighs.

I sighed, controlling my patience.

'Vasu, we hail from a small city and leave our families to go to big cities where all the people are fucking rich. They only understand the language of money.'

I realized that she had an ocean of anger within her.

'So, money is everything?'

'Yes, money and glamour!' She threw away the finished cigarette butt. 'I will have a smart and rich husband this time.'

Now I was sure that I had lost my Radhika forever. Perhaps she wasn't mine to begin with.

I redirected the car to the petrol station. The operator had refilled the diesel. I was about to pay cash, but Radhika gave him the credit card to pay.

We reached her home and I helped her with the luggage. Her mom was content, but that euphoria was missing.

Before leaving her home, I said, 'You have changed a lot.'

She passed a genuine smile and said, 'But you are still the same, Vasu.'

•

Radhika made a visit to our house the next day. Her pants were too short for a city like Jaipur. I gazed at her white, skinny legs. The pants barely reached her knees and I tried hard to not keep looking at them. I have seen many foreigners dressed in short dresses, but they never appealed to me. My mom scanned her from top to bottom and took in a deep breath.

Little Tanya was getting all the attention and everyone wanted to play with her. She, on the other hand, was focused on Hunk. She walked on her tippy toes. Hunk also started wagging his tail. It seemed both Hunk and Tanya liked each other.

Mom asked a series of questions related to her divorce and enquired thrice, 'Are you happy?'

Every single time, Radhika replied with a smile, 'I am fine, aunty.'

I understood this meeting would not last for long. I went to drop her back, but Tanya was not ready to leave Hunk. They were continuously jumping around the house.

'Why don't you buy a good puppy? Tanya seems to like dogs,' I suggested Radhika.

'Yes, I can, but I want my Hunk back.'

'Why? You can buy a more adorable puppy.'

'I can buy any puppy, but I cannot buy another Hunk.'

31

Mamaji

I went to take charge of my struggling business in Udaipur. Indian tourism had witnessed a new shift. Thailand and Kerala became the new favourite destinations over Rajasthan. After spending more than two years around Udaipur, I was now planning to shift back to Jaipur. I also wanted to add Jaisalmer to our list. It was hard to manage the drivers, save taxes and survive in the fierce competition. On a few occasions, I had even worked as a chauffeur.

One evening Kavya didi called me. 'Hey, lover boy! When are you coming to Jaipur?'

'Why? What happened? Are you coming home?'

'Yes. I will be there for Raksha bandhan.'

'Okay, I will be there too.'

'You should try to come early, Vasu.'

'Anything serious, didi?'

'Your jiju is shifting to Dubai and I will also move with him soon.'

'Wow! It seems everyone is going around the world. I'm the only one who is stuck in Rajasthan.'

'Do you also want to shift to Dubai? We can try to find a job for you there?'

'Then who will take care of the families?'

'*Families?* So, you are counting Radhika's family as well?'

'She is not doing well. She needs me, didi.'

'I don't think so.'

'How can you say like that, didi?'

'Have you seen Radhika's Instagram pictures?'

'I checked her profile last month. She was not active on Instagram.'

'You can check now. And remember, we do not stalk, we research.'

I laughed. I logged into my Instagram profile and checked Radhika's photos. My eyes widened upon looking at her profile. She had posted pictures in shorts, hot pants, backless crop tops, and other fashionable dresses. She looked like a glamorous diva in all of them. There was only one picture of Radhika with Tanya and it had the least comments. She had not posted even a single picture in traditional clothes. I scanned a little more and found one picture where she was wrapped in a black saree and wet untied hair. I could see her belly and naval so clearly. My attention then got diverted to the backless blouse. I could see her glowing skin. I stopped blinking my eyes for a few seconds.

My intense desires had suddenly woken up. The breath was heavy and I noticed that something was rising under my pants. For the first time, I wanted to meet Radhika, but for different reasons. I checked her profile summary. She had more than four thousand followers and every photo had more than a thousand likes. The shorter the dress, the more the likes!

In one picture, Radhika was flaunting her naked and seductive back. It had 455 comments and I tried to read a few of them. All the comments were by males sending kissing emojis. Some wrote – *looking hot, so sexy* and one comment even said, *you made me horny*. I wanted to kill that man. I closed Instagram. I couldn't understand how two years of married life had changed Radhika so much.

Soon, I went to Jaipur. Kavya was coming in the late afternoon so I thought of visiting Radhika in the meantime. I got the update that her mother's health had deteriorated further and the frequency of dialysis had also increased. Radhika opened the door, wearing pink shorts and a thin t-shirt. She looked stunning with her shining skin and perfectly toned body. I had hardly noticed her dress, but the effect of Instagram had started winning over me.

I called out to Hunk and Tanya came almost running. She had recognized me. Hunk followed her, jumping with joy. It looked like I had found my lost family. I gave the candies which I had brought to Tanya.

Radhika's mom came to the living room and smiled. She playfully asked Tanya, pointing at me, 'Tanya, do you know who he is?'

The little girl replied, 'Vasu!'

'No! Mamaji.'

'Mummaji!' She only managed to speak that much.

'No, say ma-ma-ji,' aunty guided Tanya.

I rubbed my face and lowered my gaze. Tanya clung to my phone, she wanted to play games. I unlocked the screen and gave it to her. Radhika was in the kitchen all this while.

'When will you shift to Jaipur again?' Her mom asked, settling down on the sofa slowly.

'I am trying, aunty. Anyway, nothing is happening in Udaipur. Tourism is not that great these days so I might return soon.'

'Hmm, you know I am on dialysis and I have less time to live.'

'Don't' say that, aunty. You will get better soon.'

'Have you seen the changes in Radhika?'

'Yes, she has become more active on Instagram.'

'What is Insta....Instagram?' she struggled to pronounce the word. I understood that we were not on the same page.

'Vasu, I am trying to convince Radhika for a second marriage, but it is hard to make her believe in love again.' She passed a frustrating sigh. 'She has lost faith in relationships. Sanju was an abusive man and indulged in extramarital affairs. It is hard to believe that such things happen even in love marriages.'

'Oh, so it was a love marriage?' I asked sarcastically.

'Yes, of course, they studied together. I thought you knew that.'

I wanted to say that I have also studied with her.

'Vasu, you are the only one I can ask. Help her to find a suitable boy.'

'But how can I help her to find a boy?'

'You are just like her brother. Isn't that the reason you are helping her?'

I went silent and frowned. It seemed that my fate was playing games with me. Just then, my phone buzzed. Tanya dutifully gave it to me.

'Hey, where are you, lover boy?' she asked.

'What happened? Have you reached home?'

'Yes, and please don't go to meet Radhika.'

'Why? What is so special?'

'If you go there, you will be bro-zoned for sure.'

'Bro-zoned!' I whispered.

'You idiot, today is Raksha bandhan!'

Radhika walked in, holding a tray of sweets and *sharbat*. My eyes flickered. I rubbed my eyes and cleared my vision.

'Radhika, today is Raksha bandhan and Vasu is here.'

I pouted like a flop actor and took a deep breath. I was sitting in a dangerous position. Tanya was on my lap, playing a game on my mobile and my one-sided love was about to be strangled by a rakhi.

'Radhika, you can tie a rakhi to Vasu.'

I rolled my eyes and prayed to all the gods I knew.

Radhika neared me. I closed my eyes and thought she was about to do the blunder, but she lifted Tanya from my lap and said, 'Mom, stop it! He is my friend.'

'Friend!' her mom made a face.

'My only friend.'

'He is mama,' the cute Tanya blurted.

32

The Best Option

It was a pleasure having Kavya in the house. This time, she was staying for a longer time as her husband had moved to Dubai and she was taking a sabbatical from her bank job. I had hardly used her bed, laptop or dressing table while she was away.

I woke up one morning and found her doing yoga. She had put on weight and had now stopped eating junk food. I had never thought that she could sacrifice samosa, pizza, kachori or even vodka.

Mom secretly updated me that she was three months pregnant. She told me that I was not allowed to share the news with anyone. I wondered why she was so secretive about her pregnancy. However, I guess there was one full-grown baby in the same house already. After all, she always treated me as if I had stopped growing.

The same night, Kavya asked about Radhika's well-being and declared, 'Lover boy, she is not the same girl anymore.'

'Yes. Now she is divorced.'

'I am not talking about her relationship status, Vasu.'

'Then?'

'Her behaviour, her way of talking, and her body language.'

'Seems like you are stuck on the body more. Change is inevitable. She had faced so much in life, didi.'

'You are not seeing that which I can see.'

'What is that?'

'She is not the same innocent and sweet girl. She is... tainted.'

'Tainted. How?'

'She drinks and smokes?'

'You also had been doing that. So?'

'Are you trying to defend her?'

'No.' I raised my hands.

'Have you seen her dressing sense?'

'What's wrong with her dressing sense? Many tourists walk freely in the city wearing clothes even shorter than what she wears.'

'Oh, my little boy.' She rolled her eyes and flushed, 'Why are you so nice to her?'

'Because I like her.'

'Ok, but *why* do you like her? Give me one simple reason.'

'When I see her, a smile comes naturally on my face. I forget all my troubles. I am better with her.' I took a pause. 'I don't know why I like her, seriously.'

She raised her eyebrows and gulped.

'Okay, let's play KBC.'

'KBC as in Kaun Banega Crorepati?'

'Yes. You need to ask what kind of men she wants to get married to and you need to give her four choices.'

'Out of the four choices, one would be me?'

'Yes, Vasu!'

'When there are options, no one would choose me, didi.'

She gave a congenial smile and placed her hand on my shoulder. 'But you said, you like her so she also has to like you.'

'Why? It's my love for her. It's okay if she doesn't like me.'

'Then there is no future.'

'But I never cared for a future with her anyway.'

'It is all good when you are young without any responsibilities. But with time, you have to be responsible. You have to take care of families and you need to plan your future.'

We both gazed at each other.

'If she fails in operation KBC?' I asked doubtfully.

'Then you need to leave her forever and settle with me in Dubai.'

I tried hard to absorb her thoughts. Suddenly, there was silence in the room. I looked at her; she was waiting for my answer. I nodded after a few seconds. I picked my mobile phone and typed a message.

Vasu: Radhika, I am planning to shift to Udaipur. I will be leaving on Sunday and I might return after a long time. Can we meet tomorrow evening for dinner?

Radhika: Why dinner? We will drink and party!

Vasu: Nice, be free tomorrow.

Radhika: Venue?

Vasu: How about the Trident hotel, opposite Jal Mahal?'

Radhika: Oh, the same hotel where we had my birthday party? I have some great memories there.

Vasu: Yes, it's time to rewrite memories.

Radhika: Sure. Can Tanya join too?

Vasu: She is always welcome.

After my chat with Radhika, I had a sleepless night, my mind thinking only about her.

Was I getting too involved with her? I have my whole life ahead and it was time to make a decision. Then my heart reasoned – *she is not even aware of my feelings. Was I doing the right thing? Does she care for me? Was I just a friend or more than that?*

I picked my phone, opened Instagram and looked at her pictures. There was a smile on my face and suddenly it felt like she was mine. I put the phone aside. With a contented heart, I dozed off.

Next day, I picked Radhika and Tanya from their house. She was dressed in a short, sleeveless printed dress with a low cut neckline and constricting bodice. The dress clung to every curve of her body. From the dress, bold red lipstick to high heels – everything was highlighting her. I was so mesmerised that I kept gazing at her whenever I could.

We reached Trident hotel. It was the same place where I had gifted Hunk to Radhika. We walked into the same restaurant. Radhika, Tanya and I sat in the same corner. Last time, Sanju was sitting in the middle, and this time, it was Tanya. It looked like life had given me one more chance.

'Do you remember the place, Radhika?'

'Yes, it was my best birthday.'

Little Tanya was happy to explore the ambience. She asked for my mobile to play games and I gave it to her.

The waiter came with a suggestion, We have a separate playing area for children. There's an attendant there too, if you want to drop her there.' I looked at Radhika.

'Good idea!' Radhika said.

We walked to drop her at the playing area. Tanya was excited to see the playing lounge. There were several big and small soft toys, a huge Mickey Mouse and air-filled swingers. The hygiene and safety gears were all in place. The manager pointed at the CCTV stating that everything was under control and strict supervision.

Once we made sure that Tanya was safe and playing happily, we returned to our table.

'What would you like to drink?'

'Whatever you order,' she said teasingly.

I eyed the waiter and asked, 'Do you have Black Dog whiskey?'

'Yes sir. Nice choice.'

The waiter served the drinks with complimentary snacks. He started serving in two glasses.

'Wait. I will not drink. Give me a grape-wine mocktail instead,' I said, stopping the waiter.

'What is this, Vasu? It's not fair.'

'I need to drive back, Radhika.'

She rolled her eyes and flushed. We raised a toast and she gulped the first peg down like fruit juice. Then, the waiter filled the second glass. We sat there for a few minutes, talking about my tourist business.

She pouted and her wet shiny lipstick seemed inviting to me. I shifted my gaze and sighed. She lit a cigarette and started smoking like a carefree woman. Soon, she was two pegs down. I instructed the waiter to play some peaceful music. He changed the music and suddenly, there was so much peace gazing in the air.

She finished the third drink and the smile on her face widened. I understood that I could start preparing my ground.

'So, Radhika, are you ready to marry again?'

She lit her third cigarette and said, 'I am ready to marry a hundred times.' Meanwhile, the waiter made the fourth peg. 'What happened? Why so serious?'

'I am thinking of what to talk about.'

'Don't think, my friend. Just go with the flow,' she said with a drawl.

'No. Let's do something different. Something that we have never done before. Let's play a game.'

'Game? Really?' Her eyes widened. 'You can play with Tanya. She will be more than happy.'

'What about playing KBC with me? Kaun Banega Crorepati? I will ask a few personal questions and will give four options. You need to choose one.'

'Okay, sounds interesting,' she said excitedly. 'I am ready to play any game which is going to make me rich.'

'You have to be honest in the game, Radhika.'

'Fine. Let's begin the game,' she said in high spirits.

'Which city is your favourite? Your options are – Jaipur, Delhi, Hong Kong or Chandigarh?'

'Hong Kong.'

'Why?'

She took a sip and gave a cold stare. 'Here, people judge me and they think that I am hungry for sex. When they see my pictures, they make a negative opinion about me. So, I challenge them by putting seductive pictures. I want them to burn in their envy.'

'Good answer! Now, time for the second question.'

'Go on! I am enjoying this game, Vasu.'

'Suppose you get to live a different life, which life will you choose? And the options are Miss World, a police officer, a doctor and a scientist.'

'Of course, Miss World.'

'Why?'

'I will have a million followers on Instagram.'

'I never thought that social media followers were so important for you.'

'Yes. They appreciate my pictures and I am in their dreams. It's so amazing to see people respect you.'

'Have you seen how a patient reacts when a doctor saves their life?'

'Fuck, I don't want to save any life, Vasu.'

Her eyelids were heavy. I understood that it was time to ask the right questions.

'What kind of husband do you want? And your options are – a loving person, a rich person, a good-looking person or the best friend.'

She flickered her eyes and pouted like a cute doll. She asked to repeat the options. I understood that I had asked a tough question. I explained again and she said, 'Can I choose more than one answer?'

'Yes, you can.'

'I want to marry a rich and good-looking person.'

I shrugged. She understood that I had demanded an explanation.

'An average-looking boy can only invoke sympathy within you.'

'Is being handsome so important to you?'

'Vasu, only a rich and handsome man can make the world jealous. Your appearance prevails eventually.'

'You have changed, Radhika.'

'Yes, and the only person who hasn't change is you, Vasu.' She winked.

I stared straight into her eyes, without blinking. My eyes welled up, but she was too drunk to notice.

'Now my turn,' she said.

I gave a nod.

'Suppose you have to choose a partner? What kind of girl would you choose?'

'Where are my options?'

'Same option as yours. A beautiful one, loving, emotional or rich?'

I started laughing like a fool. It looked like she was drinking and the effect was over me. She demanded an answer.

'Radhika, I only had one option. And now, I have lost that also.'

33

The Hint

I left for Udaipur to expand our business. As a travel entrepreneur, I had discovered a new version of my personality. I was able to take our endeavour to new heights. I had blocked Radhika from all social media platforms. I wished I could block her from my life too. I stopped asking for anything related to Radhika or her mom. I used to come back home once in a month, but I eventually stopped it altogether to avoid meeting her.

Meanwhile, Kavya kept sharing her baby bump pictures on WhatsApp. She was five months pregnant. She kept asking when I would be settling back in Jaipur, and every time, I would make some excuse. I did not know whether I was running away from something or chasing a bigger purpose. But deep down, I wanted to go home.

Soon, we entered the year 2020. It was the most difficult year for us. A new virus had hit China and many European countries had started withdrawing their travel pursuits. The tourism business was stuck. I concluded the operations in Udaipur and returned to Jaipur. Perhaps, I was running away from myself because I preferred to stay back.

Many drivers were leaving and returning to their home towns. I was struggling to pay them. Driver Bablu had already left for Bihar at the last moment and there was no one around. So I decided to take up the role of the chauffeur. I went to the airport to receive the guest with a placard that said – WELCOME AJAY K PANDEY.

I greeted him with a smile and he reciprocated warmly. He was carrying a cabin bag and his pleasant aura. As I escorted him to the car, he occupied the front seat. Soon, we headed towards the hotel.

'Sir, what is the plan for the day?'

'Actually, I need to visit a bookstore and in the evening, I may visit the Udaipur city.'

'Okay, so you need the booking for eight hours?'

'Ten hours, I suppose.'

'Sir, you have come here for work or vacation?'

'Both actually. I am an author.'

'Author?' Suddenly my perspective about him changed.

'What kind of books do you write?'

'I have written eight books around love and relationships.'

'Wow, eight books!'

I raised my eyebrow and looked at him from top to bottom. I had imagined authors with heavy spectacles, grey hair, dark circles and wrinkled faces. I had never thought that an author could be so smart. I parked the car outside the bookstore which he had mentioned. We had reached ahead of his scheduled time. He remained seated in the car, busy sending messages to someone. My curiosity compelled me to strike a conversation again.

'Could you tell me the names of your books, sir?'

He listed all the titles, but I could only register *The Best Wife* and *The Best Friend*. They were very relatable.

I realised that he could be a the person who could help me to calm my restless mind.

He finally went to the book launch. I turned on the air conditioner and lay back on the car seat, thinking about my family and then, Radhika. Trying to forget someone you love is like trying to remember them strongly. The harder you try, the more you fail.

Mr Ajay came back after two hours. As soon as he sat in the car, I asked, 'Sir, what is the next location?'

'Let's go to the city palace.'

I drove to the city palace. Udaipur was not a big city. There was enough time for him to explore. I asked while driving, 'Sir, I need a piece of advice.'

'Sure, how can I help you?'

'Sir, I like a girl but I can't decide whether she is a perfect partner for me.'

'Are you in a relationship with her?'

'Yes, as a friend. But, I am still wondering if it is the right relationship or not?'

'Any relationship which doesn't make you a better person is the wrong relationship.'

His philosophy was hard to register. I rubbed my forehead and asked another question. 'What do you mean by "a better person", sir?'

'If you are happy, forgiving and doing something selflessly, then you are a better person.'

I never thought life was so simple. It took some time to absorb his thoughts. I dropped him outside the City Palace museum. He returned after an hour, with a congenial smile on his face.

'Let's go to the hotel, Vasu.'

While we were heading towards the hotel, I asked, 'Sir, I felt cheated in a one-sided relationship. What should I choose – forgiveness or revenge?'

He furrowed his brow for a split second and then, passed a wide smile. He asked, 'How can you be cheated in a one-sided relationship?'

I rubbed my chin. I had never thought about it in that way. We had reached the hotel and before I could say anything, he suggested, 'Come to my room and we can talk more.'

'How do you know that I want to talk to you?'

He smiled and said, 'I cannot leave you with that cliffhanger.'

I followed him. I thought he was a rich man and would be staying at some luxury hotel. But, he was staying in a small room in a two-star hotel. I sat on the small uncomfortable sofa and he sat on his bed.

'Could you tell me about your problem, Vasu?'

'I love my best friend and because she doesn't love me back, I have blocked her from my life. I don't know whether I have done the right thing or not.'

'So, you are struggling between love and revenge?'

'Revenge? Not really. I mean, how?' I held my chin.

'Breaking a friendship is a kind of revenge. So, you need to choose between love and revenge.'

I nodded.

'Suppose you break this relationship and move on. Will that make you happy?'

'Yes.'

'No, Vasu. You will be happy for a few days, but then you will start cursing yourself. If you forgive her, then you will be in pain for a few days, but later on, you will smile and sleep peacefully every night.'

'So, what shall I do?'

'I don't know. But in a one-sided relationship, revenge is not an option.'

'It is hard to decide, sir.'

'When it is hard to decide, then go and stand in front of the mirror and ask the question to yourself, you will get the answer.'

'If I don't get the answer. Then?'

'Keep on asking the question. One day, the inner voice will give you a hint. You need to be smart enough to comprehend the hint.'

'I feel like....she doesn't like me?'

'Has she told you that?'

'No, but I know that I am a below average looking boy. And, any girl will hardly choose me if they have any option.'

'Did she say that you are not a good-looking boy?'

I shook my head.

'This is your inferiority complex which is overpowering your mind. The negative judgments that you have faced all your life has made you believe that you are not good enough. It is not true. Remember, if you can be a friend, you can be the best life partner as well.'

I tried to make sense of what he was saying. His words echoed in my mind and heart.

'I am still confused. Please suggest me something.'

'You have to find your own answer. Remember, commit to yourself. Because even if you fail, you have no one to blame and if you succeed, you know how many sacrifices you had to make to reach your destination.'

I scratched my jaw and narrowed my gaze. His philosophy confused me more.

•

The next day, it was hot and sunny. I decided to take an early shower as I was feeling sweaty. I undressed and went to the washroom. I stood under the shower and got lost in the cool water. I was recollecting the events of the day and a thought came to mind. I stepped out to look at the washroom mirror. I saw a dark man with white teeth.

I asked the person in the mirror, 'Was it the right decision to block her?'

There was no answer from the other side. I asked again and no one replied. I shouted again, 'Was it the right decision to block her?'

I stopped asking. I gritted my teeth and washed my angry face in hopelessness. I finished taking the shower and before leaving the washroom, I gazed at the mirror again.

My eyes landed on the chest where there was a tattoo and a small, red-coloured heart. The name "Radha" was written. Her name was still in my heart. I smiled with joy and contentment.

Finally, the mirror gave me a hint.

34

Second Chance at Love

I came back home after the longest gap. Mom and dad were immensely delighted to see me and Kavya taunted, 'You finally remembered that we exist!'

'Sorry, didi. I was busy with work.'

'Don't try to act smart with me.'

I passed a smile. The more you love, the more it gives you the right to ridicule.

Kavya had turned into a full rounded doll and her baby bump was easily visible. I never thought she could carry so much weight, but she was looking cute. I had never seen all these things so closely. I wished I could also be a father someday.

Only those who travel outside would understand the importance of home. It was an amazing feeling to be with my family. The same evening, when I was getting ready to go out, Kavya said, 'Don't go to meet her.'

'Why?'

'Her wedding is fixed.'

'Don't make things up to dissuade me, Kavya. I know you don't like her.'

'Don't be a fool again, Vasu.'

I did not believe her. I purchased chocolates and a balloon for Tanya and walked towards Radhika's home. Her mom opened the door. Tanya was also there to greet me. Before I could say anything, the cute little Tanya started shouting for the balloon. She was more interested in the balloon than me. I gave her the balloon and she demanded the chocolates too.

I walked inside in excitement to see Radhika after so many months. She was sitting on the sofa with a middle-aged, smart-looking man. He was resting his chin on his hands. He was wearing a dark-coloured coat and black shining shoes. His smile, attitude and flawless face revealed that he was a wealthy man. Now, I understood why Kavya was trying to stop me.

Her mom introduced both of us. 'Vasu, meet Karthik, Radhika's would-be husband. This is Vasu, Radhika's childhood friend.'

Radhika was pleased to see me. She neared and nudged me on the shoulder.

'Where did you vanish so suddenly? Why was your phone switched off?'

'Actually, I had lost my phone and got a new number.'

'What happened to your WhatsApp and Facebook?'

I could not answer and she did not seem to be interested in knowing the reason. However, I was happy that there was a smile on Radhika's face. Her mom went to the other room.

'Let me make tea for you,' Radhika said and went to the kitchen.

Karthik and I were alone in the hall. There was an awkward silence between us. I eyed him from tip to toe and passed a smile.

Karthik asked after a fleeting formal smile, 'How is your business doing?'

'All well.'

'Radhika always talks about you. You have been a good friend to her. Thanks.'

He reminded me of Sanju who had said the similar words at the airport.

I asked, 'So where do you live, Karthik?'

'My house is in Malviya Nagar in Jaipur but I am settled in Hong Kong. After the wedding, we will shift to Hong Kong or Singapore.'

'When is the wedding?'

'Next week.'

'Congratulations!' Everything seemed to be happening so fast.

'How did you guys meet?'

'We met on Instagram and I liked her pictures. I texted her and she replied. After a long chat and a couple of meetings later, we decided to move ahead.'

'So fast?'

'Yes. Everything happened in just two months.'

'Can I ask a personal question if you don't mind?'

'Yes, please. Feel free.'

'Why did you decide to marry her?'

'Actually, I am also a divorcee. I was looking for someone with the same profile. It would be easy to settle down. I found her attractive and she also liked me.'

Radhika walked in with three cups of tea, cookies and a huge smile on her face.

'Hey, I need to go,' Karthik said, getting up to leave

'What about the tea?' Radhika asked.

'You know, I don't drink tea. I need to go. I had a good time with you all. I should take your leave now. Vasu, do come for the wedding.' With that, he left in a hurry.

Radhika and I were left alone in the hall.

'I wanted to inform you about the wedding, but you suddenly vanished from my life.'

'Congratulations, Radhika! You are getting married for the second time and I did not even get a single chance.'

She laughed and I joined too.

'You are too fast and furious,' I remarked.

'Yes, Vasu. Consider this an arranged wedding. He liked me and we met twice. I found him to be a nice man. So, I agreed to settle with him.'

'Yes, he is smart, handsome and attractive. It is like the union of two most attractive people.'

'Yes, he is.'

I decided to leave the place. I walked towards the exit and she followed me to see me off.

'Thanks Vasu for helping me a lot.'

I did not say anything.

'Now don't go missing till the wedding.'

'Actually, I may miss the wedding as I am going to Dubai.'

'Can you not postpone it?'

'No, not this time.'

'Try if you can.'

'Actually...' I looked straight at her face and said, 'I don't want to try.'

•

I rushed to a liquor shop and bought the cheapest whiskey and a bottle of soft drink. I emptied half of the soft drink and mixed it with the whiskey. I drank almost half of the bottle in one gulp. I blinked my eyes and cleared my vision. It felt suffocating. I threw the empty bottle and walked towards home.

I halted near a paan shop and chewed a strong-smelling mouth freshener. I went straight to my room upon reaching home. Kavya was lying on her bed, on a video call. I silently settled down on my bed.

Kavya ended the call and said, 'So finally, she is getting married again?'

'Yes!'

'I told you.'

'Not in a mood to discuss, didi.'

'Come here! I know you are drunk and why.'

I shook my head.

'Come here please, Vasu.'

I did not reply and continued to rest on the bed. I had so many queries running in my mind. Then, I realised that I knew the answers to them already.

I hugged my pillow and wondered if I could either fight with someone or talk to someone to vent out my emotions. I opened my eyes and shifted on to her bed. I closed my eyes, and she stroked her hand over my head. The television was on as she was watching some daily soap.

'I want to go to Dubai, didi.'

'So, you finally lost the battle?'

'I was never a contender in the battle, didi.'

'But you never told her that you love her. She is not even aware of your feelings.'

'It is just one-sided love.'

Kavya suddenly unmuted the TV to divert our attention. They were running an interview with the actress Nandita Das. Her words echoed in our silence.

The advertisements of fairness products and remarks about one's complexion can get 'dangerous'. Women suffer from such low self-esteem due to these ads. It is not just about putting nail polish or external beauty. It is telling you that you are not good enough so you can't get, a husband, a job and you are going to make your parents sad. It is like doomsday.

'See they are saying that fairness cream are encouraging racism,' Kavya said.

'What the hell is this? Can we switch off the TV?' I yelled.

Kavya switched it off.

'Don't lose your patience.'

'I want to go to Dubai. I hate this racist place.'

'So, you have started hating India now?'

'Go to any matrimonial site, go to any hotel front desk, see any newsreader, go to Facebook and Instagram, you will find only good-looking people. A fair-skinned girl will get married twice and a dark-skinned girl has to face seven rejections.'

'Don't blame the country because of a frivolous lady.'

'But, are we responsible for our complexion?'

'Do you seriously need an answer?'

'No, didi. I don't need anything.'

'You need peace.'

Tears welled up in my eyes. 'Can I hug you, didi?'

'Oh, Vasu!'

I hugged her and whispered, 'I wish you are blessed with a boy. Because if you have a girl and her skin tone is dark, you will have a difficult time. A boy like Vasu can struggle, but I don't want a girl like Kavya to suffer.'

35

The Confession

After having a long discussion with Kavya's husband, I booked a flight for Dubai, two days before Radhika's wedding. Jiju had arranged a short-term work visa for me. There was no confirmed job, but I was keen on making a fresh start.

All the Rajasthan tourist operations were handed over to dad. He decided to sell a few old cars and only focus on Jaipur and Agra.

It was the evening before my departure. Every news channel was flashing the breaking news that Narendra Modi would address the country today. It had to do with the recent virus spread in China. I switched off the TV. I hated those news channels. They were showing the same news repeatedly. I guess I started hating everything around me.

'Vasu, you are not going to meet her for one last time?' Kavya asked.

'No,' I responded sternly.

'I'm talking about Radhika's mom.'

'She is on dialysis and you know the reality.'

'Oh!' Somewhere in the process of hating Radhika, I had stopped caring about others.

I regretted how I had avoided Radhika's mother when she was sick. I sat on the sofa with a heavy heart and took in a long breath.

An image of her mother, struggling to breathe flashed in my mind. I regretted why we have a brain which could imagine everything and make the situation worse. I concluded that it is important to be a good person rather than a failed lover.

•

When I reached her home, I found a car parked outside. I had seen that car before, and knew that it belonged to Karthik. I understood that I was unwanted and went to the other side of the lane. I had masala tea and smoked a cigarette after a long time. While returning, I crossed the same lane again. The car was gone, so I bought a few candies and rang the bell. Radhika opened the door.

'Hey, how are you? I was thinking about you.'

She was wearing a slit Kurti with a blue-coloured body-hugging denim dress.

'How is your mom doing?'

'She is not well but she would be happy to see you. Just a few minutes ago, she was talking about you with Karthik.'

I did not understand why Karthik was mentioned in the conversation.

The beautiful princess came panting to see the visitor and Hunk started wagging his tail. I realised how I had started liking Tanya more than Radhika. She never discriminated because of my skin-tone. If I loved her, she loved me back. I wished she would never grow up. However, today she looked a little drowsy. I pulled her up and embraced her.

'Be careful. She has been vomiting since morning,' Radhika said.

'Shall we take her to the doctor?'

'We just came back from the clinic.'

'Okay!'

'What did you bring for me?' Tanya asked.

I gave Tanya her favourite candies and then, I noticed that she was already holding one big chocolate in her other hand. But still, she wanted more. She reminded me of little Radhika.

'Who gave you this chocolate?'

'Daddy.'

I rolled my eyes, regretting my decision to visit her house. Then, I walked swiftly to see Radhika's mother. She was lying on the bed with a content smile. How could she smile even after facing all the adversities?

'How are you, aunty?' I asked.

'I am fine, Vasu. When are you leaving for Dubai?'

'Tomorrow.'

'At least you could have waited for three more days. We have arranged a small wedding for Radhika.'

I pouted and unfolded my arms. I passed an expression that I am helpless. Suddenly Tanya started fidgeting on my lap.

'What happened, Tanya? All well?'

She coughed and vomited on my shirt.

Aunty screamed, 'Radhika, Tanya has vomited again.'

Radhika came running, holding a towel and cleaned up Tanya. She made Tanya lie next to her mom and shouted in an authoritative tone, 'Don't move, Tanya! And no more candies!'

'Shall we visit the doctor?' She shook her head.

'Radhika, give one of your father's t-shirts to Vasu,' aunty said.

'No no, aunty. I am fine.'

After a few seconds, Radhika came back with a shirt. I tried hard to deny, but she insisted so I went to the wash basin and removed my stinking shirt. I was still wearing my cotton vest when Radhika came with a sanitizer spray and said, 'You can spray it on your body.'

'Hey, not required, I am fine.'

She frowned and gazed at me. I noticed that she was looking at my chest.

'You have a tattoo?'

'Oh, it's nothing. It is just a silly tattoo,' I said, hiding it.

'What is written there?'

'Nothing, Radhika.'

'Seems you have a secret girlfriend.'

She gripped my vest and I tried hard to stop her. It was too late. She gazed down and appeared to be stupefied.

After a few seconds, she said, 'Who is Radha?'

'A friend...'

'You never talked about her.'

I went silent and left the place. I wanted to run out of her house. I waved goodbye to Tanya and said to Radhika's mother, 'We will meet again for sure, aunty.'

'Take care, beta.'

I stepped out and found Radhika waiting in the drawing room.

'Now I know why you are running away from the wedding.'

I gazed down at my feet, not knowing what to say to her.

'I want to talk to you.'

'Please take care, Radhika.'

She stood there between the door and me.

'Who is Radha?'

I sighed, tightened my fist and closed my eyes.

'Who is Radha, Vasu?'

'Radha was my friend. I have always loved her. I loved her since I was a child. She was the only girl who sat with me on the back bench in the class. My Radha had rejected to become a queen if I could not be the king. She was the girl whom I wanted to marry. But somewhere in this corrupt world, I lost my Radha. I could only see Radhika everywhere.'

My eyes welled up and my breath was heavy.

'Why did you never share your feelings with me?'

'I wish I could and I tried many times. But somewhere, I realized that you have so many options! I was not even on the list.'

'You are always important to me, Vasu. Always.'

'Anyway, it is all useless now. Soon you will fly to Hong Kong and tomorrow I will be in Dubai.'

'Does that mean we are meeting for the last time?'

'I have thought many times in the past that it was our last meeting, but destiny always brought you back,' I said and smiled sadly. 'Only to be taken away later. We will meet again for sure.'

'You believe in destiny?'

'Never! But when things are beyond your control, we need someone to blame and I decided to blame it on destiny.'

'You have always helped me. Is there anything I can do for you?'

'Yes! Be happy wherever you are. And try to be a better person.'

She nodded. I was trying hard to control my emotions. Her nose turned red and her breath was heavy.

She stretched her arms. I hugged her for a few seconds and then she whispered, 'You never changed, my friend.'

We freed ourselves from the hug.

'But you have changed, Radhika. You are not the same. I have seen multiple versions of your personality – a cute angel, an adult innocent Radha, Mrs Radhika, divorced Radhika and the rebellious Radhika. Soon, you will be the married Radhika again. You have faced so much in life and still, you have not stopped living. You have become stronger.'

'Sorry, Vasu.'

'No need to say sorry. Your name is already tattooed around my heart.'

'But I wish I could...' She choked.

'Don't worry. Remember Krishna had sixteen thousand gopis, but he could never marry his Radha.'

36

The Hopeful Stars

The same night, PM Narendra Modi imposed nationwide lockdown to fight against the COVID-19 virus.

On 25 March 2020, the first day of the lockdown, nearly all services and factories were suspended. All the schools, railways, airlines, cinema halls, public gatherings, private offices were closed for the next twenty-one days. There was an immediate restriction on travel. And, air travel was banned.

I got an email stating that my Dubai flight was cancelled and I could postpone my travel without any extra charges.

I read the news and shouted, 'This is not fair! Now I would be here to attend her wedding.'

There was a strange smile on Kavya's face.

'Why are you smiling?'

'God always gives you a hint,' she said and winked.

'Why does god have to drop hints all the time and not say things directly?'

'He will, if you believe in him.'

'I don't believe in unrealistic things.'

'When you were praying for your Radhika, then you used to believe in such *unrcalistic things*.'

I rubbed my hands over my face and we stared at each other. I decided I should not argue with my six-months pregnant sister.

The next day, my mom visited Radhika's home. She returned with a disappointed expression.

'What happened, mom? Are you okay?' Kavya enquired.

'Radhika's wedding has been postponed by two months because of the lockdown.'

'Why have they postponed it for two months?'

'They are not sure about how long the lockdown would last. The next auspicious date is after sixty days.'

Kavya looked at me. We did not say anything, but I understood what she was trying to communicate. I could see the naughty grin on her face. She moved to the kitchen to get more details from mom. I went back to my room and switched on the TV.

Kavya returned with a lot of information. I knew she was dying to share the same with me. I was sitting silently, and she sat on my bed, looking at me. We looked at each other for a long time, but none of us breathed a word.

'Do you want to ask me something?' Kavya finally asked.

'Not at all. Nothing related to Radhika.'

She rolled her eyes.

•

The lockdown started and we remained indoors, looking at the fan, walls or TV. Sometimes I went to the terrace to get some fresh air. but there was no physical movement beyond that.

Our entire life, we begged for free time and suddenly, there was so much free time that we didn't know what to do with it.

I found a few old people as well as new faces in our colony. People had now started covering their faces with protective masks. Every conversation was about the invisible virus that had transformed our lives.

A group of Italian tourists were diagnosed COVID positive and Jaipur was declared the red zone. It meant more restrictions. I was confined in the house and Kavya was the only person with whom I could talk and vent out my frustration. Only essential shops selling groceries, milk and medicines were open.

I could easily go and meet Radhika, but I avoided it. Almost every morning, my mom went to Radhika's home and returned with Tanya and Hunk. Tanya was the only one who helped us smile for a few hours during the lockdown.

One day, when I woke up and switched on the TV, I saw a shocking news.

Actor Sushant Singh Rajput had committed suicide at the age of 34. The actor was found hanging at his Bandra residence. A mental health professional was sharing information on mental illness and how depression was a hidden disease. His untimely death had unsettled the entire nation.

•

I was always grateful that I was staying in Radhika's neighbourhood. It was funny that few blessings were turning into a curse.

One day, Radhika came home, alone. I was a little taken aback. She was wearing shorts that had slits at many places. It felt like a rugged fishing net. Her red coloured t-shirt was too big for her but I assumed it was some fashion trend that had never made any sense to me.

Mom sighed, scanning her from bottom to top and welcomed her. Papa was lost as he was waiting for international flights to resume soon. He was worried about the tourism business.

We sat in the lobby and there was an awkward silence.

'Where is Tanya?' mom asked her.

'She is sleeping, aunty.'

Mom did not say anything, but I was sure she was silently wondering what Radhika was doing here.

'I have come to meet Vasu. I was getting bored.'

Mom passed a smile. She picked up the remote and switched off the TV. Papa wanted to protest, but mom silenced him with a statement.

'We have run out of essential items in the kitchen, and you only care about the news.'

Papa passed a smile and followed mom to the kitchen. I was sitting silently. I was a little uncomfortable even though I had spent almost my entire childhood sitting next to her.

She shifted a little closer to me. I fidgeted as if something dangerous was nearing me.

'I want to talk to you.'

'You wish to talk to me only because you are getting bored?'

'No, it was the official reason.'

'What is the real reason?'

'I am confused.'

'Why are you confused?'

'About the wedding.'

'Yes, even I am wondering why you postponed your wedding. Fifty people are allowed for the wedding, which is enough in your case.'

'I am confused about the wedding, not about the number of wedding guests or arrangements.'

'I am not getting you.'

'I am not sure if I am ready. Or if he is the right man or not?' she said like she was purchasing an insurance policy.

'I am leaving this country, so who will help you if you get confused next time?'

'Next time? Vasu, there will be no next time.'

'I am sorry. I meant you have to manage on your own now.'

'You are talking as if we will never meet again.'

I wanted to say yes, but remained silent instead. I looked at the centre table and the transparent water bottle was half-filled. I had a few sips of water and smartly avoided her question.

'So, why are you confused about Karthik? He has everything you wanted in a man – money, looks and confidence.'

'So, now you know what women want.'

'No, I know what my friend wants.'

'I am happy at least we are still friends.'

'No one can take that away from me. It was all I ever had.'

'And now suddenly, you are so confident?'

I shrugged.

'Maybe this lockdown is turning me into a philosopher.'

'Are you fine, Vasu?'

'What do you think?'

'You sound so different.'

'I am not the same person anymore.'

She blinked her eyes in confusion. I was not making sense, it seemed.

'Vasu, put yourself in my shoes and see. What would you have done?'

'It's difficult to imagine being in your place. No one can do that.'

'But what if I am confused in life? Who can I discuss my dilemma with?'

'You were always so clear in your thoughts. You always knew what you wanted. How is it possible that *you* are confused?'

'It is possible! We are humans. We change with time and circumstances.'

'So, what do you want from me?'

'I need your advice. I am tired of posting my pictures on Instagram.'

I nodded.

'Should I marry Karthik or not?'

'Do you love him?'

'I don't know! I guess I just like him.'

'Then why are you getting married?'

'Because he said he loves me and he proposed to me.'

'I guess it's okay that you both like each other. What else do you want?'

'But there is no love; I am confused. What if I stop liking him tomorrow?'

'Oh my gosh!' I laughed. 'Why don't you buy an insurance policy? If you both stop liking each other, the insurance company will pay you a big amount.'

Her eyes went wide. 'What is wrong with you?'

'Are you looking for a guarantee in a relationship? What if you love someone today and stop loving him tomorrow?'

I sighed and took a long breath, mumbling, 'I am not the best person to advice you on this.'

Suddenly Kavya walked in with drooping shoulders. I could easily guess that she had a tough day.

'Can I check something with Kavya?'

I shook my head in disbelief.

I stood up from the sofa. My face was stiff and I was trying hard to control myself. I sat near her and almost gave a cold look as I said, 'Radhika, I have faced enough. You are a part of my best memories. But I have convinced myself this time. You went away last time and it hurt. I know, you will go again. But now I have changed. I am not the same stupid lover anymore. I know that I am depressed, but I can manage.'

•

There was a small puja at home, but mom did not invite anybody as the government had restricted any social gatherings. I had refrained from attending the ceremony. Kavya called me during the aarti, but I made an excuse and went to the washroom.

Kavya had offered homemade milk cake as prasad. I took it with care, but when no one was watching, I threw it in the dustbin. The same night, when Kavya was cleaning her bed, she bent down to throw some unwanted papers in the dustbin. She eyed the dustbin and screamed at me.

'What happened?' I yelled back.

She pointed at the dustbin. I did not give any explanation. She was so angry that she stopped talking to me.

It was late in the night. I switched off the lights and was getting ready to sleep. I assumed that Kavya had already slept by now. I picked up my mobile and opened the video apps, scrolling for some video.

'Don't watch the video in the dark. It will harm your eyes,' she shouted.

'Oh sorry! I thought you were sleeping.'

'How can I sleep so easily?'

I switched on the light and found my sister, looking at me with burning eyes. I felt bad. I had never asked how she had been dealing with her pregnancy issues. I neared her and said, 'I am sorry, didi.'

'Why are you saying sorry?'

'Because I threw the prasad in the dustbin?'

She smiled. 'Why are you losing hope, Vasu?'

'I know what you want to say. But I am done, didi.'

'Her wedding got postponed just a day before the scheduled date and your Dubai plan also got postponed. Now you are stuck here for more than a month.'

'I don't understand all this.'

'These are hints in which you have stopped believing.'

'What do you want me to do?'

'Why don't you try for the last time?'

'I am tired, didi. Please do not push me.'

She pulled a paper and pen and started thinking about something.

'What happened? What nonsense are you planning this time?'

'Mind your own business.'

'Why are you doing all this?'

'When the sun goes down, the stars come out.'

'What does that mean?'

'You are tired, but your sister is not.'

37

The Right Question

Kavya Speaks

It was lockdown. My husband was stuck in Dubai. I was with my loving family. However, nothing was more painful than watching my best friend and brother so badly wounded in love.

I often believed that Radhika was not the same person whom my brother had loved all through his life. She had changed a lot. She was posting revealing pictures and her WhatsApp stories were often about her smoking and drinking parties. It looked like she was taking revenge from the entire world. I knew that divorce had broken her, but still, she was the only girl for my brother.

I had noticed a few changes in Vasu. First, he had stopped believing in god. And then, he had filled himself with anger and resentment. Whenever I asked for the TV remote, he would give it easily; when I ordered him to bring me some water, he would go silently. He stopped fighting with me. He just lay on the bed and watched movies on Netflix.

He asked about depression and suicide that made me extremely scared. My patience had reached its peak when I found the prasad in the dustbin. I concluded that I needed to act before I lose an innocent soul. I had to plan something before he did something stupid.

When the lockdown ended, Vasu was in a hurry to book the tickets to Dubai. He was in Jaipur only for a few days. I started inquiring about the options before he left the country. I understood that forcing anything on him would be useless. He had given enough to this one-sided relationship.

One evening, Tanya came home with mom, and I noticed that there was a smile on Vasu's face. He had a special connection with her. It was the same pleasing smile which he had for Radhika when she was a kid. I comprehended that when you love kids, they will love you back with all they've got.

So later that day, I went to meet Radhika. She opened the door, dressed in red cotton hot pants. 'How are you Kavya?' she asked, smiling.

We walked to the drawing room and I saw Karthik already sitting there. Radhika joined him on the sofa.

'Hey Kavya, how are you doing?' Karthik asked the same question.

When you are pregnant, everyone will keep asking the same question.

'I am doing good, thank you. How is aunty doing?'

'She is stable, but not in a great condition.'

'I have come here to invite all of you for my baby shower ceremony. It's tomorrow.'

'Oh, that is great! But I am sorry I won't be able to make it,' Karthik said.

'Please Karthik, you have never visited our house, so you have to come.'

'Sorry, but I have a meeting.'

Karthik denied my request for the second time. I gazed at Radhika and made an emotional face, which could even melt Hitler.

'Just try if you can make it for a few minutes,' Radhika said.

There was something magical in Radhika's request and his expression changed.

'Okay, I will try to come for a short while.'

'See you tomorrow at 5 p.m. then,' I beamed.

'You are leaving now? Let's have tea or coffee?' Radhika offered.

'No, I need to do some preparations for tomorrow.'

'You came just to invite us?'

'Yes.'

'You could have called. No need to be so formal.'

'No, I wanted to meet aunty as well.'

'Oh! So, how many people are coming?'

'Only a few important guests are invited.'

My eyes landed on Tanya. I picked her up, settled her on my lap and asked, 'Tanya, my princess, which kind of toffees do you like the most?'

'Orange candy,' she replied adorably, stretching her palm.

'Sorry, Tanya. I don't have the candies right now. But tomorrow I will give you lots of candies.'

•

'How many guests are coming?' Mummy, papa and Vasu asked twice about the function. I told mom that only a few guests were coming. It was more like a bachelorette party and not a traditional baby shower.

My mom narrowed her eyes. The worry line on the forehead said it all. And after a few seconds she asked, 'What are you planning?'

'I want an empty house.' She looked at me wearily.

'Actually, we just want to celebrate with friends.'

'Okay, we will go to the temple at that time.'

'Good,' I said almost casually.

'But please don't drink.'

I smiled at my mom's assumption. I instructed Vasu to shop for a packet of orange candies, juice, some dry fruits and sweets. He helped with the decorations.

A few hours later, we were all set for the evening party. I sat on the single sofa and realized that I was missing something.

'Vasu, can you purchase a toy or a teddy bear?'

'Why so many things?'

I did not answer. Mom and dad had already left for the temple and I was getting nervous. I assumed that mom and dad would not come for the next one hour.

I messaged Radhika on WhatsApp that we were waiting for her and Karthik. She replied that she would be coming in a few minutes.

'Who will be coming today, Kavya?' Vasu asked.

'Radhika is coming.'

'Why have you called her? Why do you want me to face her?'

'I cannot explain it to you.'

'No, you have to or else I will leave the place.'

'No, Vasu. I need you.'

The doorbell rang and the attention was diverted towards the guests. I opened the door and welcomed the three guests – Radhika, Karthik and Tanya. They looked like the perfect family. A pang of guilt ran through me. I wondered whether I was doing the right thing.

'Vasu uncle,' Tanya shouted.

Vasu greeted them with a fake smile and walked silently to his room. I guided them to the drawing-room.

'Nice house,' Karthik said.

'Thank you.'

'So where are the other guests?' Radhika asked.

'I invited so many people, but because of the lockdown and social distancing, everyone refused to come.'

Radhika nodded but doubt clouded her face.

'Thanks for coming Karthik.'

'My pleasure! But I need to leave in half an hour. I took a small break from work.'

I nodded. Thirty minutes were enough for me. I went to the room and saw Vasu burning in anger.

'You have invited Karthik as well?'

'Vasu, you can get angry and fight with me tonight. But right now, I need you outside. Please serve the snacks to the guests and sit with us for a few minutes.'

I went back to the drawing room. There was no music, no dance and no religious formality. They both had worry lines on their forehead. I was amazed as there was nothing to talk about.

We were smiling and exchanging gazes at each other. And then, Karthik asked, 'Where is Vasu?'

Vasu arranged the table with refreshments. The menu was simple – soft drinks, salty snacks and assorted sweets. I lit a diya, played a religious song, and requested everyone to pray to lord Krishna. They followed my instructions. I understood one thing – when you have no clue, just turn to god.

'I need to leave, Kavya,' Karthik said after a few minutes.

'A few minutes more,' I said.

I checked the seating arrangements. Radhika was sitting across me on a single sofa. Karthik was sitting on the left side and Vasu was sitting on the right on a single chair. Only Tanya was running around in the entire house.

I called Tanya and said, 'Let's play a game.' Tanya came running towards me.

'I will give you one task. If you do it well, you will get an orange candy.'

Tanya nodded excitedly.

I pulled out two coloured pencils on the table and asked, 'Which is the red one?'

She picked the red pencil and I gave her the candy. She smiled with delight.

Tanya had seen the bundle of orange candies and she got tempted to have more. I placed a mango and an orange on the table and asked, 'Which is the good fruit?'

She picked the mango and I gave her the candy. She demanded more.

'Now tell me, who are these three?'

I looked at them – Karthik was getting impatient. Tanya pointed at Karthik and Radhika and said, 'Daddy, mommy,' and then she pointed at Vasu and said, 'friend.'

'Daddy?' I asked.

'She calls Karthik daddy. Mom made her call so,' Radhika explained.

I gave her two orange candies. 'Tanya, another question. Whom do you love more, mumma or daddy?'

Tanya looked at Radhika and Karthik and said, 'Mumma.'

'Go and give this candy to mumma.' She obeyed.

I asked her the last question, 'Tanya, whom do you love more? Daddy or the friend? Go and give the candy to the person you love the most.'

Tanya looked at her daddy and then, the friend. With small steps, she started walking towards Karthik. Then she turned and looked at Vasu. He smiled at her and then, something unexpected happened.

She turned around, walked towards Vasu, and said, 'I love my friend!' She lovingly gave him the candy.

It was hard for Vasu to control his emotions. He said, giving the candy back.

'No, Tanya. Sweetheart, you need a daddy. You don't need a friend,' he said and left the place.

Karthik stood up from his seat. 'I need to leave. Thanks for inviting me.' He left in frustration, leaving Tanya, Radhika and me alone in the hall. I gave a toy to Tanya and she was happily engaged with it.

I looked at Radhika. She asked, 'What is all this about? What are you trying to say?'

'Have you noticed why Tanya chooses Vasu over the so-called "daddy"?'

'A kid choosing someone over a candy is different from choosing a life partner.'

'Of course, it's different. Adults have to think about money, looks and many other things, but kids take a decision based on pure love.'

She became thoughtful. I understood that I should leave her alone for a few minutes. I excused myself and went to the washroom.

When I stepped back in a couple of minutes later, Radhika's facial expression had changed. It looked like I had hurt her feelings.

'Can I tell you a story about Krishna and Radha?'

She nodded.

'It is believed that lord Krishna used to love only Radha and his flute more than anything else in his life. It was his musical talents which attracted her love for him.

'This is why he used to keep the flute with him all the time. Radha married someone else. During old age, after retiring from all the duties, Radha went to meet her Krishna for the last time. When she reached Dwarka, she heard about Krishna's marriage to Rukmini and Satyabhama, but she did not feel sad. When Krishna saw Radha, he was joyful.

'Radha was lonely and weak in her last days. Lord Krishna came in front of her for the last time. Radha said that she wanted to listen to his flute for the last time. Krishna started playing a harmonious tune.

'Radha's soul left her body while listening to the melody. Lord Krishna could not bear Radha's death and broke his flute as a symbolic ending of love and threw it into the bush. Since then, Krishna has not played the flute or any other instrument for the rest of his life.'

'What are you trying to say?' Radhika asked.

'Do you love Karthik?'

'I like him?'

'Does Karthik love you?'

'Yes, just like a good friend. But we would develop deeper bonds once we will marry.'

'You don't have strong feelings for Karthik, but Vasu is your best friend. You know how much he loves you.'

'But ...' she went speechless.

'Many people dream to marry their best friend.'

'I am totally blank, Kavya.'

'I can understand you are confused. But you really don't know what you want?'

'I am not sure. But do tell me what you have in mind.'

'I think I can help you find the right answer.'

'What is the right answer?'

'Right answer is always hidden in the right question.'

'Question? What kind of question?' She interjected, seating unsteadily.

'Why are you getting married? Is it for sex, or companionship or a stable life? Maybe ask yourself, why you think you cannot settle with Vasu? '

'Why are you beating around the bush?'

'It's your life and you need to make a decision.'

'What if I decide to not choose Vasu?'

'That's your decision. Tonight, just ask yourself, why do you love your mom?'

'From where did my mom come into this?'

'The purest love in the world is what a mother has for her child.'

She went silent for a few seconds and said, 'What if I still choose Karthik over Vasu?'

'Perfectly fine.' I rubbed my palms and took a deep breath. 'Go and marry whomsoever you want, but Vasu will always love you. However, he cannot play his flute again.'

Her jaw fell and she swallowed hard. She took a long breath and had a glass of water.

'No, I was just trying to say he loves you more than Karthik.'

'Do you think it's so simple?'

'Yes.'

'When is Vasu leaving for Dubai?'

'His flight leaves day after tomorrow at 5 a.m. He might leave for the airport at 1 a.m.'

Radhika nodded and screamed. 'Tanya, let's go home!'

I went to see her off. She turned around at the threshold to say, 'Since you have quoted Krishna, let me tell you that Radha never married Krishna.'

'Neither you are Radha, nor is Vasu Krishna.'

38

The Path of Confusion

Vasu Speaks

It was a restless night as I was constantly tossing in bed. I gave up on my sleep and I sat on my bed. I looked at my phone, which had zero notifications. It was 1 a.m.

I looked at Kavya who was sleeping soundly. I opened my WhatsApp, then Facebook, and lastly I started scrolling through Instagram. I checked my feed and saw a few beautiful ladies who were showing their moves and a few boys who were sharing funny jokes. I was dumbfounded to see the number of clicks and comments on them. I zoomed in a few clicks and was amazed to notice that Instagram was filled with good-looking people. Suddenly I had noticed a familiar face. She was, and is, my favourite person.

I scrolled down and, noticed her short pants. I scrolled up and saw her body-hugging dress and her luscious lips. I exited from Instagram and switched off my cell phone. I rubbed my hands, put them on my eyelids and took a long breath.

I gazed again at Kavya and found that she was snoring at a high decibel. I decided to walk out and slowly opened the door so as not to disturb Kavya. I walked a few steps and noticed that the TV was on. Papa was watching some news channel. He noticed my presence. He fidgeted a little and got a bit uncomfortable. I was giving him a look and then wondered about what was so special on television at this hour.

'Hey, Vasu, what happened? You are also not sleepy?'

'No!'

'I know.' He took a pause and said, 'I had noticed that.'

He muted the TV and invited me to sit on the sofa.

I sat near him. He picked up the remote and switched off the TV. There was absolute silence for a few seconds. I had never been alone with him, especially like this.

'What happened, Vasu?'

'Nothing.'

'Are you alright, beta?'

'I am fine.'

'Then, why are you depressed?'

I gave him a surprised look and frowned.

'How do you know that I am... depressed?'

'That is not important. Why are you depressed?'

I took in a deep breath as if experiencing the pain all over again. 'I feel sad here. People criticise me. I feel secluded because of my dark complexion and ....'

'And ...?'

'I feel insignificant; no one wants to be my friend. No one wants to be associated with an ugly face. Everyone is obsessed with external beauty.'

'So, that is the reason you wish to leave the country?'

I nodded.

'But still, you are loved by your family. And have a good friend in Radhika.'

Something hit me upon hearing her name. I thought of changing the subject. I regretted why I had even discussed it with papa.

'I guess I would find a better job in Dubai.'

'What if you slap someone in Dubai at your workplace?'

'Oh, you know about that?'

He smiled like James Bond who knows all the riddles from the beginning.

'I know everything about you, my son. But I wanted you to learn from your own struggles. I want you to grow as you beat all the challenges that life throws at you.'

'So, did I do well?' I sounded like a confused trainee.

'No, not yet.'

'Why?'

'Because the real problem is not with people. The fault lies in how you perceive yourself.'

'What does that mean?'

He chafed his eyes, took a long breath in, and passed an endearing smile before speaking. 'You know, I have spent my entire life in the tourism industry. Every day, I meet a different foreign tourist. Most of them are fair-skinned, but they never treated me poorly. They always sat and spoke with me. I had also met a few dark-skinned Americans and Africans. I presumed they'd be living with an inferiority complex because of their skin tone, but they were always so confident. I wondered why we are so obsessed with our complexion and why they didn't give it as much thought. My mind was baffled with this query for quite a long time and lastly, I got my answer.'

'What is the answer, papa?'

'They *believe* that they are second to nobody. That's the secret. Once you are confident about yourself, no one could make you feel less.'

'So...' I ate up the rest of the words as my mind started putting the pieces of the puzzle together.

'So, the real problem is with how you view yourself in your mind.'

I took a deep breath. Then, I laid back on the sofa and smiled, thinking about him. I wanted to say I am proud of you, dad. But I did not say anything. I just sat there silently. I wanted to hug him and cry, but I don't know what stopped me.

'I guess something else is causing you pain right now?'

'Yes, dad. I don't know why people don't value us. Even those who are close to us.' I blurted out my frustration.

'Sometimes we are so accessible to them at all times that they take us for granted.'

'So, we should maintain a distance from them?'

'Can you, if they are so close to you?'

'Then how would they realize our worth?' I scratched my forehead.

'You can take a small break, but remember, we can have only a few good friends.'

'Hmm.' I breathed deeply and said, 'There is one more reason for me to move to Dubai.'

'Finally, how smartly you're justifying your relocation.'

We smiled. I looked at his serene face and couldn't fathom if I was talking to a friend or my father.

'But papa, can I ask you something?'

'It seems so many things have been bothering you for days. Where was I when you were caught up in all these issues?'

'We both were busy handling our respective business.'

Papa nodded and let out a relaxed breath.

'This lockdown has given us time to fix so many things,' I philosophised. 'Did you not feel bad that so many boys had rejected Kavya?'

He opened his mouth to speak, but then shook his head. He picked up the water bottle from the centre of the table and had a few sips. Then he said with a stiff face, 'You have no idea how it felt.'

'But you never spoke about it.'

'Poor men end up sulking in silence.'

'Why are we so helpless?'

'Son, it is the worst feeling for me to experience when any Tom, Dick or Harry comes to my house, eats my snacks and dares to judge my daughter for her looks. It burns me.' He covered his face with his hands for a moment and then said, 'I was so helpless upon seeing all this. You have no idea how I felt.' He pursed his lips and grunted to clear his throat.

'If you had such strong feelings about it, why did you keep inviting such people home?'

'Now, I realise that it was a mistake. I guess I failed her as a father. I was unable to give this confidence to my daughter that she is perfectly fine. She is no less than any other girl.'

He started trembling. His voice was shaky, and he was clearing his eyes. I shifted a little close to him and put a hand on his shoulder.

He looked at me with teary eyes. 'I failed to give this confidence to my daughter and now, my son is also facing the same inferiority complex.'

I pulled myself and hugged him. I don't know why I started shedding tears. I closed my eyes and slowly murmured, 'You have not failed, papa. I am proud of you.'

•

It was 1 a.m. Mom and dad had slept and I had sought their blessings before they retired for the night. Even then, mom had asked Kavya to wake her up when I was ready to leave for the airport. Kavya and

I decided not to disturb them. I zipped up the bags and called up the driver. He was already waiting outside.

I checked the flight status and found that it was on time. Kavya was busy texting someone.

'Best wishes for the baby,' I said, hugging Kavya at the door, ready to leave.

She smiled.

There were more worries and less sadness on Kavya's face. I understood that she was busy planning something, but I decided to walk out. I opened the door. There was absolute silence in the air, but I noticed someone standing there.

I walked outside and saw Radhika, holding a polybag.

'What are you doing here so late? It's not safe.'

'I thought I'd see you off till the airport.'

'Who told you about the timings?'

'Kavya told me.'

I looked at Kavya, thinking why she needed to make this difficult. But it felt nice that my best friend was there.

I kept the luggage in the boot. Radhika and I left for the airport. I looked at Kavya and waved goodbye. She smiled and waved back.

When the car had driven more than half a kilometre, I asked, 'What are you holding in your hand? If it is for me, then give it to me na!' I teased.

'Yes. This is for you. It's a little goodbye message that I will show you when you are about to enter the airport.'

'Why so?'

'You always welcome me at the airport. I thought I should see you off with a placard sign.'

She sounded mysterious. 'Can we play KBC? I will ask a few personal questions. I will give you four options and you need to answer.'

'KBC? Why so? Are you trying to trick me?' I knit my brows in confusion.

She smiled. 'Here is your first question. What can stop you from going to Dubai? The four options are – stay here for the family, for your Radhika, for yourself and the last option, no one can stop you.'

'Nothing can stop me,' I replied.

'You know when you played that KBC trick and asked a question about what kind of men I want, I was drunk and confused. You did not even give me any lifelines.'

'Lifeline for what?'

'In KBC, there is a lifeline – phone a friend. If I had chosen that option of calling a friend, I might have made the right decision.'

'But you were never confused.'

Radhika smiled and came closer to me.

'Vasu, I have met all kinds of men. They were handsome, smart and rich. I got married to one and you know the rest. People who are known for their looks are less known for anything else. Last night, I thought about my happy moments and all of them were with just with one person. I was always smiling with my best friend.'

I swallowed the tears welling up in my eyes and stared at her. I was pondering on what to say when the driver said, 'Sir, we have reached the airport. Shall I park in the parking lot or just drop you here and go away?'

'You wait in the parking for Radhika ma'am.'

I carried the big bag with Radhika's help to the airport entrance gate.

'Now beyond this, I need to walk alone.'

'Are you going to miss me?' Her smile was full of sadness.

'That question holds no value.'

'Anything you wish to say?'

'Just be happy! Believe me, it feels amazing to see your best friend happy in life.'

She nodded and we hugged. I stepped back and gave a nod with a complementary smile. I turned and walked to the entry queue. I knew Radhika was standing and waiting for me to enter and I did not wish to see her.

My mind said, *you are meeting her for the last time*. I summoned the courage and turned to look at Radhika. She smiled and pulled the paper from the polybag, displaying the A4 size paper.

I narrowed my eyes and read the penned message – *I love you, Vasu*.

A smile spread on my face. I left the queue and walked towards her.

'Don't do this! Go, marry and live a life of a queen! I have nothing to offer. This is not the face you wish to see every day. Don't take your decision out of sympathy, Radhika.'

'This is the only face which I have been seeing till now.'

'Don't do this. You went away so many times and it hurt. It kept hurting. I know you will go again.'

'I went without a friend.'

'What is so special this time?'

'Every girl has a wish to marry someone who loves her unconditionally. Just like you!'

'So, you need a friend, or a husband?'

She gazed down in an awkward silence.

I pursed my lips, took a long breath and tried hard to control myself.

She smiled amidst tears and said, 'I never thought a best friend could be a good husband. I need a man with a kind heart.'

'But you always wanted a handsome man.'

She looked at her feet and mumbled, 'Yes, I do.' She took an effort to speak. 'Last night was tough for me and I kept on asking why I loved Sanju? Maybe we get attracted to a beautiful face first and then, we start spending time with the person and end up loving them.'

'Nothing wrong in that!'

'Yes!' She shook her head. 'I went to see my ailing mother. She was in deep pain. Last night was a difficult one for mom. I was hurt upon seeing her in such a condition. I gave her a painkiller and sat silently until she slept peacefully. I read her face and realized how much I loved her. I hugged her softly. I came back to my room and wondered why I love her? She is not the most beautiful woman on this earth according to what society would like to believe.'

Her voice trembled. I put my hand on her right shoulder and asked softly, 'So, what does that mean?'

She raised her face and gave a firm look. She spoke softly, 'If a good-looking face was the definition of beauty, then no one would have loved their ailing mother and wrinkled father.'

'What made you change your mind?'

'It took me one divorce and two breakups to realize this.'

I stepped forward and closed my eyes. We hugged each other warmly.

She whispered, 'You are the most handsome man for me, Vasu.'